There in the dried ~~leaves lay a~~ ed
Young. Shapel

With her emerald ~~eyes~~
got shakily to her ~~feet~~
over to him on ba~~re feet.~~ ~~on~~ opened his
mouth to ask a question, freezing in shock when
she stood up on her toes and covered his mouth
with hers.

Instant, raging desire. His body, so long without
sexual release, reacted even as his mind shouted
out warnings.

"No," he snarled, pushing her away. Breathing as
hard as he, she stared at him. A second later, her
face contorted as if she were in pain.

"I'm...sorry." The words came out in gasps.
"Please, leave. Now, before I do something else I
can't control. I'm...burning."

Then, as she took another step toward him, he
realized she meant with need.

Sexual need.

What little control he'd had over his own arousal
vanished.

KAREN WHIDDON

Though she doesn't howl at the moon, Karen Whiddon swears she can sometimes communicate with wolves' close relatives—dogs. Her two fur-faced children are her closest friends. Having grown up in the Catskills and the Rockies, she enjoys shadowy forests and snowcapped mountains. Her hobbies include camping and fishing. In addition to writing, she works full-time as vice president of a commercial insurance agency and makes her home with her wonderful husband and two canine companions.

You can contact Karen by e-mail via her Web site, KarenWhiddon.com, or by snail mail at P.O. Box 820807, Fort Worth, TX 76172.

CRY OF THE WOLF

KAREN WHIDDON

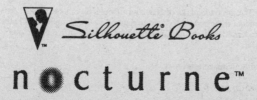

Silhouette Books

nocturne™

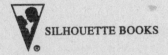

SILHOUETTE BOOKS

ISBN-13: 978-0-373-61754-8
ISBN-10:   0-373-61754-2

CRY OF THE WOLF

www.silhouettenocturne.com

Printed in U.S.A.

Dear Reader,

Though the closest I've ever come to being around wolves is romping with my two miniature schnauzers, *Cry of the Wolf* is a story very close to my heart. The abuse and battering of women has reached epidemic proportions in the U.S., and many people don't quite understand the low self-esteem that is a result of such constant belittlement. I do. A lifetime ago, I, too, was involved in such a relationship and I also blamed myself. Convinced for several years it was all my fault—after all, as he'd said, if I'd been a better wife he wouldn't have had to hit me—I finally pulled myself up from the floor and left. Somehow, despite the death threats and the stalking, I was able to move on and make a new life—the same as Jewel fights to build in this book. I hope you enjoy her story as she moves toward her own new beginning with Colton Reynolds, hoping for a life full of happiness—exactly like the one I now enjoy.

Sincerely,

Karen Whiddon

To my daughter, Stephanie, who realizes
what kind of life she doesn't want to have.
For her work with children and her constant goal
of self-improvement, I want her to know how proud
I am of her and how much I love her.

To my editor, Natashya Wilson, whose brilliant
editing made my last book much better and who
cheers me on and is always positive.

And lastly, to my husband, Lonnie,
for being all a man should be.

Chapter 1

Jewel Smith slipped from her dark rental house and padded across the dewy lawn. Dawn crept across the velvet sky, tinting the night with subtle trailers of rose and amethyst. Soon, the awakening sun would blaze over the horizon, shooting flashes of light off the unruffled surface of the lake.

Tranquil. Quiet. A perfect time for a new beginning. If she could manage to slow her heart rate and still the fine tremors that shook her.

Even though she'd escaped, even though she had her freedom, she was still trapped. Trapped inside a body being torn apart, a body where one half warred with the other.

Though her new life had begun the moment she'd fled, she wouldn't consider herself truly living until she could once again *change*. Her other self, residing inside her always, howled restlessly, insistently, for release. The wolf needed out. Shifting from human to wolf was such an integral part of her that she'd die if she couldn't do it ever again.

She could no more stop trying than she could stop breathing.

Slipping through the trees, avoiding an intricate spiderweb glistening with morning dew, she came to the edge of the still water. Out on the main body of the lake, the bass boats were already gathering, the fishermen intent on their lines. None had entered her sheltered cove. Perhaps the fishing was bad in the water near her cabin.

To make certain she would have privacy, she'd spent the past two mornings out here, hiding in the trees, observing, watching for intruders. Paranoid, because Leo had made her that way. Alone, because she'd be dead if she trusted anyone from her old town. And damaged, knowing she had to get up the nerve to try to shift, to become her other self, the sleek and deadly ivory-coated wolf.

Fingering her long silver wolf necklace, she

trembled, remembering. The last several times she'd attempted to change, the war raging within her body had become worse, as had the pain. So far, she'd survived, though the raging urges that shook her could find no release. She wasn't sure how much longer this would hold true. Changing was absolutely vital to her continued survival.

Somehow, though she wasn't sure what he'd done to her, or how, she knew Leo, her ex-husband, was responsible. Hadn't he told her often enough he wished her dead?

But he'd taken such pleasure in her suffering; she'd known he'd keep her around until she went stark raving mad. And beyond.

At least now, she didn't have to endure the violent rapes when she was too weak to defend herself.

Or the beatings. Or the…

She shuddered, stopping her thoughts. She was free now, finally clear of a man she recognized as inherently evil.

But his evil still tainted her, lingering on her skin, in her blood. She was a shifter who could not shift, a broken woman who refused to give up. Truthfully, she had no choice.

Closing her eyes, she took a deep breath. The air's heavy humidity promised the day would be a scorcher. Dipping her toe in the tepid lake water,

Jewel squared her shoulders and lifted her face, letting the breeze caress her skin. She smelled nothing but lake water and fish, humidity and freshly mowed grass.

Now. Heart pounding, she took a deep, calming breath. Then, slipping back into the concealing thicket of the trees, she stepped out of her sundress, dropped to the ground on all fours and uttered a quick prayer.

Now, she would change. She began the process tentatively, hoping for the best.

Instead of the stretch and pull of her bones lengthening, sharp pain lanced through her. Awful hurt, killing damage, as though her entire body had been caught in a rusty bear trap. No!

Gasping, she attempted to stand, to reverse what she'd begun, but couldn't make her own body obey. Desperate, she fought herself, jack-knifing as agony knifed through her stomach. Where claws should have sprung from her fingers, bright red blood oozed instead.

Inside, she felt her body tearing, something deep within ripping her apart. The pain was a slow and vicious torture. She could only hope her death would be swift and soon.

She made a small cry, knowing no one could hear her. One last shuddering breath was all she managed before the edges of her vision grayed and blackness claimed her.

The quiet moments before dawn were Colton Reynolds's favorite time of the day. The full heat of a July afternoon was still hours away, and in the faux cool, the hungry sand bass would be schooling, breaking the surface of the water in search of food. Ripe for the right lure, cast by an experienced fisherman.

A Thermos of hot coffee next to him, he eased his Skeeter bass boat from the slip of his boat dock, heading for his favorite cove at the north end of the lake.

Three days had passed since he'd been able to get out on the water; three long, miserable days spent down in Austin reporting on the latest political session.

But now, finally he was home again in Anniversary, and this was the perfect morning to catch a big, fat bass before heading off to work.

Fishing brought him the only peace he was able to find these days.

Rounding the turn to the secluded cove, he searched for the white whooping crane that had made the muddy shore its private fishing grounds. He found the bird on the other side of the bank, serene and motionless as the boat chugged toward it.

The scents and smells of the water teased his nose. He lifted his face to the breeze and took in a lungful of early morning air.

The point looked different. As he drew closer he realized the unkempt weeds and grass leading down to the lake had been freshly mowed the day before.

Something else was different, too—the old Pryor place. The run-down cabin had apparently been rented. A beat-up car, maybe an old Buick or Pontiac, was parked crookedly in the gravel driveway.

The car matched the house. Colton shook his head. He hoped whoever was living there would fix up the structure. The cabin had looked on the verge of collapse for years. He wondered how it was even livable.

Whistling softly, he cut his motor and dropped anchor. The rope played out to about fifteen feet— not bad for sand bass. He chose a brightly colored spinner lure, attached it to his line and cast, admiring the flash of orange as the lure arched across the water and dropped with a soft plop.

Contentment—or as close to that particular state of mind as he got these days—kept him still, motionless and waiting. Any moment, the sun would burst over the horizon, welcoming the day in a blaze of scarlet.

A group of ducks swam past in a loose V-formation, quacking cheerfully. He watched them while he reeled slowly, feeling the resistance the lure made as it spun a few feet below the water. The ducks went ashore in the trees near the Pryor cabin, some settling in the mud at the edge of the water, others heading into the woods to forage.

As he pulled his lure out of the water and prepared to cast again, the wild ducks erupted in a flurry of noise, taking to the water as though a saber-toothed tiger pursued them. Colton grinned, straining to see if he could catch a glimpse of what had caused such alarm. Most likely it was some half-starved cat on the prowl.

There, at the edge of the trees. Instead of an animal, he could have sworn he saw a glimpse of pale human skin shining through the unruly underbrush.

Puzzled, he set his rod and reel on the deck and pulled anchor. Starting his motor, he eased the boat closer to the shore, running aground in the soft mud. Jumping out, he tied the anchor rope around a sturdy tree and went to investigate.

Definitely a person.

Blanching, he swallowed. Took a deep draft of

air, trying not to gag. Though it wasn't the same, couldn't be the same, he couldn't help but remember Angela, his daughter. He'd found her, dead and facedown in the dirt, and the image of her crumpled body would forever be burned in his mind.

This. Was. Not. The. Same. Hell, no.

He blinked, dragging his shaking hand across his unshaven chin. Not Angela. He hoped like hell he wasn't about to stumble over the bloated body of some hapless drowning victim, just now washed up on shore. If he did, he wasn't sure his sanity would survive it.

Get a grip. He took another deep, shuddering breath. If this was a human body, he'd have to find a way to deal with it. He hadn't heard of any recent drownings or boating accidents. And as a reporter for the *Anniversary Beacon,* he should know. But what he'd seen had definitely looked like a body. What else could it be?

Pushing through the underbrush, he saw in a moment. Facedown in the dried and dead leaves, long blond hair spread around her in a tangled mess of twigs and dirt, lay a woman.

Young. Shapely. *And stark naked.*

He staggered. Nausea again filled his throat. Straightening, he cast his gaze skyward, not praying, not exactly. He could do this, he could.

He had to—no way could he leave this woman lying here, alone and unprotected. Especially after what had happened to Angela.

This wasn't Angela. His daughter was two years gone, practically the only thing remaining to show she'd ever lived a simple granite marker over her grave. His ex-wife had destroyed everything except the few photo albums he'd managed to save.

He took a step forward, pushing the past away and focusing on the present, on this woman. Was she dead? He grabbed her wrist, finding an erratic heartbeat. Alive. So far, so good.

Unconscious though. A slow trickle of blood oozed from under her fingernails, though he saw no wounds. Forcing himself to inspect her body, he saw nothing else. The woman didn't appear to be hurt in any other way.

Drunk? Drugged? Or had she been the victim of an attack?

The sight of her lying reminded him of his ex-wife's many excesses. Okay. He tried for a charitable thought, knowing not everyone was an addict or a boozer. Was it possible this woman was seriously ill? Or had she been abused or raped? The blood on her fingers could be from her attacker.

Either way, she was in trouble and needed help.

Since he wasn't a doctor or paramedic, he flipped open his cell phone to call 911.

"Don't," the woman croaked, rolling over and pushing herself up on one elbow. Dried leaves clung to her tangled hair and he fought the surprising urge to brush them away. Instead, he focused on her face. Her startling green eyes, though full of pain, appeared clear and drug free.

"I don't know. You were unconscious and—"

"Please. I'll be all right." She blinked rapidly, several times. "Other than my contacts hurting. Don't call anyone."

Slowly, he closed the phone. Something about her… She looked vaguely familiar, though he was certain he hadn't seen her around town. No one could forget a woman who looked like her. "What happened to you? Are you ill? Were you attacked?"

"Yes. No." She shook her head, sending twigs flying from her hair. "I don't know." Licking her lips, she regarded him, curiously unself-conscious about her nakedness.

Colton, however, was only a man. He couldn't help but glance at her full, high breasts, the sleek curve of her waist, her pale, creamy skin. Immediately, his body reacted. Of course it did. He'd been a long time without satisfying the most basic, human need.

Damn. He tore his gaze off her, searching for her clothes. A flash of red caught his eye. Material, in a crumpled heap a few feet away. Clothing? He went over and retrieved what turned out to be a soft cotton sundress.

"Here." Voice gruff, he handed her the dress. "Put this on."

Rather than looking grateful, her brow creased in a frown. Then she nodded, pushing herself up to her knees and dropping the garment over her head. With her emerald gaze still focused on his face, she got shakily to her feet.

"Thank you," she said, louder and more firmly this time, her voice silk and smoke combined. "I appreciate your help."

Despite the plain dismissal, Colton made no move to go. He couldn't help but notice that the simple dress, rather than disguising her lush body, enhanced her curves, making her appear even more alluring. Right. If he was young and stupid, which he wasn't.

This kind of trouble he didn't need or want. He shook his head, his body wanting otherwise. Damn and double damn.

He cleared his throat. "You still haven't told me what happened to you."

"Oh." Dragging her long fingers through her tangled locks, she continued to watch him, her look unsettling. She eyed him the way a mistreated puppy might watch an angry stranger, as though expecting a vicious kick at any moment. This woman watched him with fear. Why? What did she have to be afraid of?

Had she been raped? Or was she high on drugs?

"I—" she began, then shook her head. Her pupils dilated, she pushed herself up, padding over to him on bare feet.

He opened his mouth to ask a question, freezing in shock when she stood up on her toes and covered his mouth with hers.

First impulse—shove her away—quickly became raging desire. His body, so long without a woman, reacted instantly, even as his mind shouted out warnings.

Obviously, the woman was under the influence of something.

"No," he snarled, pushing her away, unable to keep his gaze from her ample chest and engorged nipples. Breathing as hard as he, she stared at him. Her green eyes were dark, the color of deep water during a storm. A second later, her face contorted as if she was in pain.

"I'm...sorry." The words came in gasps. "Please, leave. Now, before I do something else I can't control."

Fighting his own urges, his own raging lust, he kept his legs firmly planted. "What did you take?"

Confusion flashed across her expression. "Take? Nothing. I... Please. I asked you to go."

Was she fighting the drug, whatever it was? How could he leave her alone, when her life could still be in danger? If she blacked out again, how much time would pass before someone found her?

Short answer—he couldn't leave until he was one hundred percent certain she'd be all right.

When he didn't move, she closed her eyes, lifting her chin so that her face would be bathed in sunlight.

"I'm...burning," she said, inexplicably. Then, as she took a step toward him, he realized she meant with need.

Sexual need.

Of course, what little control he'd been able to exert over his own arousal instantly vanished.

She eyed the front of him, gaze lingering on his conspicuous bulge. "Last chance." The throaty purr was back. "Go or sate my body's hunger."

He must be insane. He actually considered taking her up on her offer. That was why they called it thinking with the wrong head. He'd gone so long without, and told himself he was used to celibacy, that he could live with that.

Now, he realized he'd been lying to himself.

"What's wrong with you?" he asked. Not wanting to, but knowing he could either retreat or capitulate, he took a step back.

At his words, horror flashed across her face. "I don't even know you." Spinning around, she made a move for her cabin. But her legs appeared to give out, and she went down. Hard.

Pure reflex had him moving toward her.

"No," she yelped. "Stop. If you touch me, I'll completely lose control."

"And we don't want that." He heard himself say. Staring down at her, lithe and lovely and as sexy as hell, he couldn't believe he was going to take a pass on what she so freely, blatantly offered. And apparently wanted, needed and couldn't control.

What red-blooded male would? He shook his head, wondering at himself, while his throbbing body urged him to touch her. Just once. To go for it and damn the consequences.

After all, what did he have to lose?

Only the lake noises broke the quiet as they stared at each other, a few feet separating them. He couldn't seem to move, to think, or to slow his racing heartbeat.

"You're beautiful," he said, feeling like a fool the moment the inane statement left his mouth.

"Go away." Struggling to her feet, she wrapped

her arms around her waist. "I can barely control my own body."

"You don't want this?" He had to ask, one last time to make sure. If she said yes, he knew he'd lose the battle, but if she said no, he'd be able to make himself leave.

No matter what narcotic influenced her, if she said no, making love to her would be rape.

"No," she said, her full lips barely moving.

He didn't trust himself to speak. Jerking his chin in a quick nod, he turned to go.

She didn't try to stop him.

Involuntarily, he glanced back over his shoulder at the woman. Motionless, she continued to watch him, the early morning sun sending shafts of fire through her long, golden hair.

Gorgeous. Pushing the thought from his mind, he climbed in his boat, started the engine and shoved off in reverse, back into the water. There, he waited, watching until she half walked, half crawled into the cabin.

All appetite for fishing completely gone, body still aching, he headed back the way he'd come, toward home.

Close call. Taking a shuddering breath as the stranger's boat pulled away, Jewel tried to move quickly for the house. Her shaky legs refused to cooperate. The best she could manage was a kind of crab-like scuttle. No matter. She'd make it. The ramshackle cabin wasn't too far from the shore.

A fire raged inside her, a need and a hunger she'd come dangerously close to loosing on the unsuspecting stranger.

Hellhounds. Not only did he think she was a druggie, but some sort of nymphomaniac as well.

She told herself it didn't matter. The only thing she could afford to worry about now was staying alive and being able to change. Anything else was small stuff, not worth the energy.

Still, the haunted look in his eyes, the raw need she'd seen in his face, lingered in her mind.

Why?

Because she recognized it. Identified and empathized with the emotion swirling inside him.

Proving again, she was a complete and utter fool.

Looking up, she saw he waited, watching her. Though water separated them, she shivered, turning on her heels and entering the cabin.

Once inside, she closed and locked the door, testing the strength of the wood and finding it lacking. Much too thin. She'd have to see what she could do about reinforcing it.

Right. As if any wood, no matter how strong

or how thick, could keep out an enraged wolf. If Leo came looking for her, this cabin would provide no protection. No protection at all against an enraged shifter who enjoyed making her suffer.

Lucky for her, Leo was safely locked away in a maximum security prison and had no idea where she'd gone. She worried that since the guards didn't know what he was, one day he'd escape. Though her body felt much the same as it did after one of his frequent beatings.

Exhausted, she dropped into a ratty old recliner that had come with the rental and closed her eyes. She still couldn't change. Trying nearly killed her. What the hell had Leo done to her? At first, she'd suspected he was doping her with pseudoephe-drine hydrochloride, an ingredient found in common cold medicine. The well-known remedy also suppressed the urge to change. Since she still wanted to change, longed to change, and couldn't, she doubted he'd used that particular drug. It had to be something else. Long-lasting and deadly.

It had been over three months since she'd vanished. Drugs couldn't stay in her system too much longer than that, could they?

She exhaled, still trembling, fingering her silver, wolf necklace for reassurance. She never took it off, not even when she changed. Luckily, it was long enough to make the change with her. The chain and charm were all she had left from the woman who'd birthed her and abandoned her at a fire station in a remote town in the Adirondack Mountains.

Pack took care of Pack, and one of the firefighters had brought the days-old baby home to his childless wife. They'd raised her as their own, teaching her Pack heritage and how to shape-shift into a wolf.

They'd become her family and she'd loved them with all her heart.

Shortly after she and Leo had married, she'd lost both her parents in a car accident. The day of their funeral had been one of the last times Leo had been kind to her.

Blinking, she brought her thoughts back to the present and trying to recover who she used to be. *Patience,* she told herself. Surely if she gave it enough time, she'd be herself again. Surely.

If not for the stranger who'd found her, who knew how long she might have lain there, unconscious and unprotected. Dangerous, especially because in this Texas town clear across the country from Leaning Tree, she didn't know her friends from her enemies. Though she'd needed to go far, far away from Leo's little empire, she knew no one here. She'd chosen this place because she'd watched a fishing show while in protective custody, and Anniversary's lake had been featured. Leo didn't know the place and hopefully he never would.

Still, she'd have to be more careful. Wincing as she rose, she headed for the kitchen to make a cup of calming herbal tea.

A reporter knew where to dig. Within minutes of chatting with Reba Mae Evans at one of the local real-estate offices, Colton learned that the woman who'd rented the old Pryor place was named Jewel Smith. An unusual first name to make up for a perfectly ordinary last name. He wouldn't be surprised to learn the entire name was bogus.

Her face still haunted him—he had seen those hollowed cheekbones and brilliant eyes somewhere before, but where? Had she been a model or an actress?

A search of public records revealed that no one named Jewel Smith held a valid Texas driver's license. No surprise there—he'd detected some kind of northern accent when she'd spoken.

Still, just to be certain, he checked criminal records next. Nothing. No reason whatsoever to suspect her of illegal drug use—except for the fact that he'd found her naked and unconscious in the woods, bleeding. From the way she'd tried to jump his bones, without even knowing him, he guessed she hadn't been the victim of a violent rape.

Here was an interesting story.

What reporter could resist? Colton smelled more than just an ordinary story. This just might be a chance to make good on his promise to his dead daughter and prevent another senseless death from drugs.

Two hours later, he leaned back in his chair and admitted defeat.

For now.

Locking up after himself, he left the newspaper office and headed home, where he planned to order a pizza, pop a cold beer and zone out in front of the TV.

When the ten o'clock news came on, Colton grabbed the remote and switched off the television. What kind of reporter was he, when he couldn't even bear to watch the news? Luckily, Floyd, his boss at the *Anniversary Beacon,* didn't know about that little quirk.

Too restless to sleep, he took the boat out instead, ostensibly to do some night fishing. He hated that he couldn't stop thinking about her.

Jewel Smith. Beautiful, sensual and elegant. Familiar. He knew he'd seen her somewhere before, but where? Where? The memory nagged at the back of his mind, but he couldn't make it come.

Still feeling vaguely unsettled, he moved across the lake slowly, his headlight cutting a wide swath in the darkness. With the wind in his face and the roaring in his ears a poor substitute for what he inexplicably craved, anger rose in him. Images of her naked, her creamy skin damp with dew, were burned into his brain. He'd been afraid to sleep because he knew he'd dream of her, sleek and sexy and moving underneath him. He both wanted her and wanted to find out the truth about her.

He was worse than a fool.

Knowing that didn't keep him from pointing his boat toward her cove.

Chapter 2

The hot and humid air made Jewel feel sticky and uncomfortable. Restless. She slipped from the house and drifted silently through the trees to the edge of the water. Here perhaps, if she sat motionless, the lake's nighttime calmness would seep into her.

Tranquility by osmosis. She could only hope.

Outside, the light breeze blowing off the lake made things slightly better, but there were other risks to ward off. She could smell the faint scent of other animals, nocturnal game prowling the still, wild woods around her. At least her shifter senses still worked, even if she couldn't change.

Above, myriad stars sparkled in the velvet sky. The moon, still full and pulsing with power, called to her other self, the missing part of her. She desperately longed for the freedom of the change, to race and run and hunt on four paws, snout lifted to taste the scent of the wind and the earth.

The ground felt solid under her feet as she walked down to a thicket of trees close to the water. But her entire body felt *wrong,* off-kilter. She was tired of fighting herself. If only she knew what had been done to her, she could find a way to purge it from her system.

For now though, she could only wait and pray.

A rabbit dashed by in the underbrush and Jewel spun, blood surging. Bitterly, she subdued the wolf, knowing she didn't dare attempt to change so soon after her last disastrous try.

In need of a distraction, she thought of the man instead. He seemed familiar to her, as if she might have met him somewhere, known him before, in another time or place.

In another life.

Shying away from the thought, she focused on his physical attributes, planning to dissect exactly what made him seem so familiar.

Perhaps it was his resemblance to Clive Owen. She nearly laughed out loud. If all it took was the look of a film star to lull her natural wariness, then she was already halfway on the road to madness.

No, the feelings he evoked in her had to be more than that. Tall, solid, with broad shoulders and muscular arms that made her think of a protector. If he were Pack, she'd have looked upon him favorably as a potential mate; especially since his size and agility spoke of a good hunter.

Potential mate? She sat cross-legged within the protective circle of trees and stared out over the moonlit water. Shaking her head at her own foolishness, she rubbed her tired eyes. Been there, done that. Not about to get back in that dance again. For a long time, maybe never. Choosing Leo as her mate had been the mistake to top all others. She would never again trust her own judgment where men were concerned.

What she'd seen in Leo had been a lie. What she'd seen as focus had truly been obsession. His cunning had become ruthlessness, and whatever kindness he'd once harbored in him had fled long ago.

Marrying him had been a one-way ticket to death or insanity.

All through their courtship and the early weeks of their marriage, he'd kept his true self hidden from her. Looking back now, she shouldn't have been so surprised. After all, cruelty and viciousness were often easily masked, especially when he'd worked as much as he did. Twelve-hour days and a lot of travel made it simple for him to hide his real nature.

And, as she'd learned too late, Leo was an especially adept liar. After all, he'd had their entire town and the Leaning Tree Pack Council completely fooled.

Once she changed again, she would be a solitary wolf, outcast and alone. Later, she'd figure out how to convince herself that she liked her life that way. For now, she'd concentrate on the problems at hand.

Staying alive and shifting again.

She sighed, pushing her hair back from her face and wishing she could taste the night air with her other, much more sensitive nose.

Dipping her toe into the warm water, she took a deep breath, hoping for peace. Instead, she saw a boat in the moonlight, moving quickly and unerringly toward her.

She slipped behind a thick oak to watch.

The boat came closer, the headlight directing a path to the shore. As the moonlight outlined the stark features of the driver, her heart skipped a beat. It was *him*.

The fact that he was here, skulking about her

place in the darkness, showed her exactly how poor her judgment had become. What was it about her, that she drew a certain kind of man to her like a moth to a flame?

Could he be a threat?

Every instinct told her no, but the possibility appeared hard to dispute. Though she hated to be always looking over her shoulder, imagining danger in every shadow, she couldn't afford to take any chances.

Leo had sworn to have her killed.

Tying the boat to a tree, the man stepped ashore and stood, facing her rental house. The moon colored his dark hair silver and made his craggy features seem even more handsome and mysterious.

Heart racing, Jewel held her breath, her entire body quivering with fury and fear. He lifted his face to the wind and for a moment she thought he'd scented her, then remembered he was only a human and couldn't. Such an advanced sense of smell was impossible for a non-shifter.

She knew he was not Pack. He smelled human. Still, was it possible he could be working for Leo? This far away?

The rough bark of the tree dug into her palms and she realized she was clasping the trunk with a death grip. Forcing herself to loosen her hold, she eyed the trespasser and wondered what he wanted. To kill her? Though she'd come halfway across the country to escape Leo, his operations had a long reach. She wouldn't be surprised to learn he'd found her. He had resources she didn't even want to think about.

Leo. Drug lord and murderer.

She thought of the last time she'd seen her ex-husband, at his federal trial on charges of drug racketeering. Aristocratic features hard and cold, he'd glared at her across the packed courtroom and loudly vowed to see her dead. He didn't understand that she'd already died a hundred times during their marriage.

Though the federal Witness Protection Program had promised to keep her safe, she hadn't trusted them. All it took was one weak link, one person to reveal the wrong fact, and she'd die from a silver bullet through the heart.

No thank you. She'd taken to the road alone, telling no one. She'd changed her name, her hair color from brown to blond and changed her style of clothing. Now, she was a new person. Only her face and form remained the same.

Touching her necklace, she tried to convince herself she'd never be found. Leo would never look in Texas—he had no reason to suspect she'd have come so far.

All she had to deal with now was the fact that Leo'd done something to her to make her unable to change, knowing she'd go mad and die. If she didn't overcome this, he'd have his revenge at last.

A movement brought her sharply back to the present, to the man prowling on her rented land, sniffing around like an untrained pup.

A quick glance assured her he wasn't armed, though she found small consolation in that. If she could have become wolf, she could have taken him easily, but as a human female she was petite and small boned, untrained in combat.

Instead of defending herself, as her every instinct urged, she'd remain hidden and watch. See what he did, what he was looking for. Maybe then she could figure out how to stop him.

Though she expected him to advance on her house, when he reached the middle of her lawn, he stopped, as still as a statue, staring at her cabin. Then he turned, looked toward the trees as if he could see her, and touched the brim of his cap in a salute.

She stifled a gasp. How had he seen her? *Had* he scented her? But he wasn't like her, and only her own kind could do that. Readying herself for combat, she couldn't believe it when instead of approaching, he climbed back in his boat, started the motor and pulled away.

Staring after his retreating shape in disbelief, she put her hand to her chest, willing her racing heartbeat to slow. Trembling and furious with her weakness, she remained behind the oak until she could no longer see him and the sound of his motor was a distant hum.

Then and only then did she step into the clearing.

What was that all about?

Disturbed and puzzled, she returned to the cabin, locked the door and slid between the sheets. The soft cotton felt rough on her overheated skin, abrasive and making her already-aching body hurt. She tossed and turned, knowing she wouldn't sleep.

Somehow, she did.

The next thing Jewel knew, bright sunshine poured through the windows and the bedside clock read 10:00 a.m.

Stretching, she woke with a sense of purpose, a renewed optimism and hope. Time to take action. If she couldn't become a wolf, she needed to learn to fight as a human. Just in case.

Even making this simple decision cheered her, made her feel empowered.

After a quick breakfast of eggs, bacon and

coffee, she did a little research. According to the phone book, Anniversary had two martial-arts studios. Jotting down both locations, she pulled on a pair of stretchy shorts and a tank top and hopped into her car. Carefully keeping to the speed limit, she headed toward town, windows open, wishing her air-conditioning worked.

By the time she reached the outskirts of Anniversary, her tank top was plastered to her back.

The first studio, located on Main Street, was in a new, white-stucco strip mall. She parked outside, watching as a class of children, all dressed in white robes, practiced their moves. Apparently, this place was popular with the under-twelve crowd. She needed something a bit more hard-edged and discreet.

Checking her notes, she started the car and headed over to the other place.

Much smaller and less flashy, Chuong's side-street location gave it less curb appeal. Here, too, watching through the large front window, she saw a class comprised entirely of younger children, but she also noticed as several women entered alone. A hand-lettered sign on the upper corner of the plate-glass window advertised self-defense classes for women. She made a decision.

Jewel stepped inside, glad to leave the sweltering heat behind her. The air conditioner ran full blast, and the cold stung her nostrils. From one extreme to the other. Standing in front of a small reception area, she rubbed her arms to keep warm.

"Can I help you?" A slender Asian teenager looked Jewel up and down, her aristocratic face expressionless. Her name tag proclaimed her to be Candy.

"I'd like to sign up for the self-defense class."

Popping gum, Candy nodded, handed her a clipboard and some papers. "Fill these out, please. Which credit card will you be using to pay?"

Credit card? Knowing how easily such things could be traced, the Witness Protection agency had destroyed all her old ones and had issued her new cards in her new name. Now, since she'd left the program, Jewel had destroyed even those. She had none. She met the younger woman's heavily made-up brown eyes and forced a smile. "Is cash okay?"

With a curt nod, Candy waved her over to a metal folding chair.

Jewel was nearly finished filling out the papers when *he* strode in. She felt him before she saw him. Crap. Her mouth went dry as she stared at him.

When their gazes met, he looked as startled as she felt. While part of her hoped he'd continue inside without speaking, she also wanted to talk with him again. Forcing a smile, she braced herself for the husky sound of his deep voice.

Instead, he continued past her with only an impersonal nod.

Shocked and strangely disappointed, she shook her head. Her entire body tingled as she stared after him.

Someone tapped her shoulder, making her jump.

"Hey, I know you." The soft drawl was familiar. Jewel frowned up at the short, curly-haired woman before recognition kicked in.

"Reba!" The talkative Realtor had shown Jewel the cabin she'd rented. She wore stretchy pink shorts and a T-shirt with the words Go for It emblazoned in neon-green across the front. "How are you?"

Cocking her head, Reba regarded her curiously. "What are you doing here?"

"Self-defense," Jewel said with a shrug. "Living alone and all, I decided I needed to learn. You?"

"The same." Reba laughed, gesturing at a cluster of other women who were busy stretching and trying to pretend they weren't eavesdropping. "We all decided to take this class when we heard about it." She leaned closer and winked. "The instructor's Max Hart. He's a hottie."

"Really?" Jewel had never met the man. "I didn't know."

"He is." Reba's grin widened. "Plus, the exercise will do us good."

The instructor came in, clapping loudly three times to gain the group's attention. He wore loose, khaki pants, a tight-fitting black T-shirt, and was barefoot.

"I'm Max Hart," he said, making eye contact with each woman. While he spoke, Jewel studied him, sizing him up. A lean, muscular man, he had that particular look common to ex-special forces. Some of Leo's bodyguards and hired thugs had come from similar backgrounds. Scrutinizing this man's face, she searched for a hint of his character, then chided herself for thinking she could tell by a simple look. What did it matter, after all? As long as he could teach and she could learn, that was all she needed to know.

"Isn't he hot?" Reba whispered.

Jewel nodded by reflex. "He's all right." While she supposed some might find his compact strength attractive, he had nothing on her handsome stranger.

Relieved her inability to change and simmering sexual need hadn't made her completely man-crazy, Jewel decided Max Hart would do as an instructor. She wondered if he gave private lessons. She wanted to learn as much as she could, as fast as possible.

But first, she'd see if he was any good.

The class began with more warm-ups and stretches. For the next half hour, Jewel learned to twist and kick and various other methods of fighting off an attack. Each woman took a turn, and Jewel saw the surprise in the hard-edged instructor's face when she effortlessly flipped him onto his back. She might not be able to change, but she still had most of her wolf strength.

Several of the women tittered nervously.

Leo would have been furious. Max merely cocked a brow and smiled, eyeing her with questions in his eyes. Holding out her hand, she helped him up.

"Very good," he told her. "Where did you learn to do that?"

With a shrug, she ignored the question, instead returning to her place in line.

"You go, girl," Reba chortled, punching her arm lightly. On her other side, two women whispered behind their hands, watching Jewel the way one might eye a particularly vicious animal.

If they only knew. Jewel flashed them a broad smile, the closest she could come to baring her teeth, amused when they instantly looked away.

A tingling on the back of her neck made her turn. Her mystery man stood in the front of the room, a towel draped around his neck, watching.

His skin shone with perspiration from what must have been a workout in the gym next door.

Had he seen what she'd done? She flushed, part of her not wanting him to know she was preparing for an attack. The other part of her, feminine and apparently completely brainless, wondered if he found her strength unattractive.

Like she cared. Focusing her attention back on Max, she decided to ignore her stranger.

Yet she knew without looking the exact moment he left the room.

Finally, the hour was up. Several of the other women decided to head over to the Mexican restaurant down the block and invited Jewel to join them. Immediately, Jewel accepted.

"Jewel Smith," Reba said, clapping her on the back. "You did well today. Made us all look like amateurs."

"Beginner's luck," Jewel said, which was a partial truth. Her unusual strength had helped, but she hadn't had the faintest idea how to easily flip a man before the class.

"You have an unusual name," one woman said. "I like it."

Unusual and pretty had been the reasons she'd chosen it. Jewel was close enough to her real name, Julie, but different enough that no search engines would turn it up. Especially with Smith as a surname. Call her paranoid, but she knew Leo's goons would still be looking.

"An unusual first name to go with an ordinary last name." A deep voice stopped her in her tracks. Several of the others twittered and giggled.

"Hey, Colton." Reba turned on the charm. "We're about to go have lunch. Care to join us?"

He declined, claiming other plans. The timbre of his voice sent shivers up Jewel's spine. Colton. That was his name. She kept her back to him, though every instinct she possessed wanted her to turn and face him, to ascertain if he was really a threat, and to defend herself if necessary.

Instead, she pressed closer into the circle of flustered women, staring at the floor until he'd moved away.

Reba noticed and slipped an arm through hers. "Hungry?" she whispered.

"Starving," Jewel whispered back. "Why are we whispering?"

"Damned if I know."

Jewel laughed, liking the other woman more and more. Though making friends had been another thing the Witness Protection Program had cautioned against, Jewel thought she and Reba might become pals.

A friend might help ease the stark loneliness of her situation. Since going on the run, she'd been completely and utterly alone. Leo had turned her into an outsider and, not knowing whom she could trust now, she dared contact no one. Her Pack back in Leaning Tree, New York, might as well be strangers. For all she knew, they considered her a traitor for testifying against Leo.

All wolves ran in packs and, since she was now denied access to both her pack and that side of herself, she needed some form of human contact.

A human pack.

Smiling at the analogy, she let Reba lead her and the others outside and down the sidewalk to the restaurant. As they reached the door, she glanced back over her shoulder.

Colton stood on the sidewalk staring after them, arms crossed and frowning.

Cheeks heating, she turned away. Her heart sank. It would be only a matter of time before he figured out who she was. Though she'd colored her hair blond and grown it long, her slender shape and unique facial features made her instantly recognizable, if the right person knew where to look. Did Colton?

Maybe making friends wasn't such a good idea after all.

"Are you okay?" Reba asked, eyeing Jewel with concern.

"Just starving." Another truth. Once inside the restaurant, the aroma of sizzling fajita meat made her mouth water. Her stomach growled, reminding her she hadn't eaten since her boiled eggs and rasher of bacon that morning.

They were shown to a large round table with mismatched chairs. Everyone took a seat, Jewel taking care to keep her back to the wall. While the others perused their menus, Jewel checked out the room. She relaxed slightly when she ascertained no threat—there were two young couples, several older couples and a few families with small children. No single men or pairs with the appearance of bodyguards or guns for hire.

The women were friendly, even though they gently teased Jewel about her northern accent. Jewel kept her mouth shut about their Texas twangs, wondering if they realized she sometimes had trouble understanding them.

She ordered beef fajitas, digging in ravenously once they arrived. Their table had gone through three baskets of chips and numerous bowls of salsa, but everyone seemed equally ravenous. Which was good, as Jewel couldn't eat slowly if she tried.

Mid-bite, she froze. She ate as though her wolf-self was coming back. She could only hope that was the case.

The bell over the door jingled and Jewel looked up.

Colton entered and was shown to a booth near the back. Jewel couldn't help but watch as he made his way across the room, pausing at a table here and there to exchange greetings.

"Popular man, Colton Reynolds," the woman next to her drawled. "Too bad he had plans."

Startled, Jewel glanced at her. On her other side, Reba elbowed her. "I think he likes you."

"Me, too," someone else put in.

"He's single, too." Grinning, Reba fluffed her unruly curls. "Of course, if you've a hankering for him, you'd better get in line behind the rest of us."

Everyone laughed.

"I wonder who he's meeting," a petite blonde named Charlene drawled. "It better not be Sue Ellen Wellman. She just got engaged to Ross Marin."

Several minutes passed while the others dissected Sue Ellen's recent engagement.

The bell jingled again. This time the man who entered sent alarm bells pealing in Jewel's head.

He looked exactly as though he could be one of Leo's lieutenants. Tall, dark and overly muscled, he had the flat, dead eyes of a man who had seen and done too much.

Jewel fought the urge to flee. She knew that type.

"Will you look at that?" Reba breathed. "Who's the hunk?"

No one knew. They all watched with open interest as he was shown to his seat, the booth in back where Colton waited.

Jewel wanted to dive under the table and hide, or better yet, make a blind dash for the door. She did neither, watching with narrowed eyes as Colton stood and greeted the man, shaking his hand before they sat.

"I'm guessing you like Colton, too." Reba's amused purr brought Jewel back to her senses. She tore her gaze away from the two men, focusing on Reba.

"I'm sorry, what did you say?"

"Colton Reynolds." Reba gave her a knowing smile. "Our favorite local reporter." Lowering her voice, Reba leaned forward. "Since you seem so interested in him, I think I need to tell you his story."

Jewel shook her head. "I'm not sure I want to hear."

"Sure you do. Why wouldn't you? It's a great story and adds to his general air of mystery."

"Yeah, and once you hear it, you'll understand

his remoteness," Charlene put in with a wry smile, stabbing her enchilada with her fork and chewing slowly.

They all watched Jewel with the avid eagerness of a flock of vultures waiting for a wolf to finish a meal of rabbit.

"I don't like gossip." Jewel softened her words with a smile. "Really, I don't."

"You'll like this. This is big."

Since Jewel knew Reba would tell her anyway, she stabbed her last bit of fajita meat and waited.

Reba grinned. "His ex-wife is in prison. And, even better, Colton made sure the woman was brought up on charges and stood trial. He refused to hire a lawyer, though she hired the best in Houston anyway. She got twenty years and her own husband put her there."

Confused, Jewel looked from Reba to the others. "I don't understand. What did his wife do?"

"He accused her of murdering their daughter. When she denied it, he set about proving she'd provided the drugs that ended the girl's life."

"Drugs?" Jewel repeated, not sure she'd heard correctly.

"Yes. The daughter died of a drug overdose. And Colton has made it his personal mission to make sure anyone involved in any way with drugs is taken down."

"Maybe that's who that other guy is," one woman put in. "A DEA agent or something. He sure looks like one."

Jewel nearly groaned out loud. Though better than one of Leo's goons, if that was the case, she knew for certain that Colton-the-local-reporter would soon identify her. Because Leo's arrest had made national news. He'd run one of the biggest drug cartels on the East Coast.

And she had been his wife.

Chapter 3

She didn't walk, she *glided.* Eyeing Jewel's beautiful, long-legged stride, Colton was aware he wasn't the only male avidly watching.

And quite possibly he wasn't the only one who thought he recognized her.

But from where? Who was she? The niggling memory disturbed him. As a reporter, usually he excelled at remembering faces and names. But not hers. He couldn't quite place her.

She wasn't a model or a Hollywood starlet. Someone else would have already matched her face to her name if she'd been prominent in mainstream media circles.

Still, he would bet Jewel Smith, with her amazing poise and beauty, had been someone the media took notice of. Had she been the trophy wife of some millionaire? He couldn't rule that possibility out. Odd how the thought of her with another man unsettled him.

Watching as she left Los Hombres Mexican Restaurant, the only quiet woman in a crowd of chattering magpies, he rubbed the back of his neck. She affected him, and he knew it wasn't merely because of her astounding beauty. There was something else, some other connection he couldn't remember. He'd have to keep digging.

The tortilla chip he'd been holding crumbled in his fingers, spraying crumbs all over the table. His lunch companion laughed.

"She's a beauty, all right." Roy chuckled, digging his own chip into the bowl of spicy salsa.

Sighing, Colton agreed. A friend from his Houston Channel Four days, Roy was in town to buy a boat. He'd called Colton, wanting to get together to talk about old times.

Colton had told him he'd come to Anniversary to forget them. Old times were all jumbled together with horrific pain. He'd agreed to lunch, as long as the past wasn't mentioned.

Roy brought up his old job before the entrée was even served. "Do you ever miss working in a larger market, like Houston? You were something else. They've tried to fill your shoes, but no one's been able to cut it. The guy working your old action segment is the fourth in two years."

"Really?" Reaching for a second chip, Colton kept his tone noncommittal. "That's too bad."

"Yeah, it is." Roy leaned forward. "Tell me you don't miss it."

"Miss what?"

"The bright lights, the notoriety. The money. All the perks that came with being a popular newsperson."

"I don't miss any of that at all. I'd prefer," he said, taking a gulp of his Corona, "to concentrate on the present."

"On this?" Roy regarded him with an amused smile, taking a swig from his own beer. "You don't even have your own local television station here."

"I like the newspaper."

"Right. How big is the circulation of that rag you work for, a couple thousand?"

"Doesn't matter." With a shrug, Colton waved

away his friend's concern. "I didn't come here for the glory. I came for the guts."

"Come on now." Tone disbelieving, the other man wiped his mouth with his napkin, motioning the waitress over for another round. "*I* work for the guts." Roy was a field correspondent for the national news. He regularly traveled into war zones and other dangerous places.

"Okay, you got me there." Colton kept his tone pleasant. "Even though my life is nothing like yours, I get my own kind of excitement here."

"Right." Roy snorted. "What kind of guts can possibly be had here in this Podunk little town? The occasional robbery? A boat accident? A bunch of tourists get too drunk and someone drowns in the lake?"

Since that pretty much summed up the stories he wrote these days, Colton didn't answer. Instead, he drained his beer and scored the last chip from the basket before the waitress set down their meals.

The food effectively distracted Roy, and for a few moments both men ate in silence.

Roy polished off his enchiladas, his taco, and the beans and rice before pushing back his plate.

Pretending not to notice, Colton concentrated on his meal.

"They sent me to make you an offer," Roy said.

Colton nearly choked on his taco. "What? Who?"

"A job offer." Nodding earnestly, Roy wadded up his napkin and tossed it on top of his empty plate. "Back with Channel Four. National exposure, with an increase in salary over what you used to make." He named a figure, the number high enough to make Colton blink.

Unfortunately, he had no need of money now.

"Once, I would have jumped at your offer," Colton began.

"Go for it," Roy urged. "Live again. Two years have passed, man. You've done your mourning. It's time to move on with your life. You can't hide out here in the boondocks forever."

Even thinking of returning to the fast-paced lifestyle he used to live made the food sour in Colton's stomach. Shaking his head, he stood, dug in his pocket and tossed a twenty on the table. "My treat," he said, moving away. "Enjoy your new boat."

Roy gave him a bemused nod, but didn't try to stop him. No doubt he—and all the rest of Colton's former co-workers at Channel Four—thought he'd lost his mind.

And, Colton thought ruefully, maybe they were right.

The newspaper offices were officially closed, due to the company picnic he never attended.

Colton let himself in, relishing the unusual quiet of the deserted newsroom. The spicy enchiladas he'd managed to choke down earlier now sat like a burning lump of coal in his stomach. As he walked toward his cubicle, he popped a couple of antacids.

The quiet of the newsroom acted like balm on his soul. Despite what Roy might think, Colton genuinely enjoyed his work now. Even before Angela had died, the pressure of his former job had begun to bother him. Now, he still got to do what he loved, though the pace was slower and the pressure nonexistent. The hours and the pay might be a lot less than what he'd been used to, but working at the *Anniversary Beacon* suited him just fine. This type of work was in his blood.

He'd come here to see if he could dig up some dirt on Jewel Smith. While he hated his unreasonable obsession with the woman, he sensed she was connected to something that just might be newsworthy. Or so he told himself. Quite honestly, he wished he'd never seen her naked nor felt the eager press of her lips and supple body against his.

Since then, she'd become a craving in his blood, a poison he needed to purge. Maybe once he solved the mystery of who she really was, he could go on with his life, such as it was.

Entering his cubicle, he turned on the light and

booted up his computer. Heading to the break room, he made a pot of strong, Cuban coffee even though he knew it wouldn't help the burning hole in his stomach. What the hell. He wasn't sleeping much anyway. Between the memories that haunted him and the woman whose face and form obsessed him, he was beginning to wonder if he wasn't a candidate for a padded room somewhere. The worst part was that a padded room was beginning to sound pretty damn good.

Jewel never knew when the urge would overwhelm her, which was in itself weird since all shifters prided themselves on their excellent control. Each child was taught the secret of controlling the beast within at an early age. She'd never had any problem controlling this before. But then she'd been able to change whenever she'd wanted.

Now, she couldn't even fall back on history. Her lessons hadn't included a situation like hers. She didn't know of any shifters who couldn't change.

After lunch, Jewel headed to the grocery store to pick up some supplies. The small supermarket was crowded with tourists and locals alike. She grabbed a basket, humming to herself as she stocked up on supplies for her cabin.

Then, in the meat department in the midst of

choosing a thick, juicy T-bone, the wolf inside made a desperate lunge for freedom. With a sharp gasp, Jewel fought it.

Falling to her knees, head back in a wordless scream, she thrashed against an invisible enemy. It never was pretty when she tried to subdue her other self.

Other shoppers stared, a small child began shrieking. One or two got out their cell phones and dialed 911.

Somehow, Jewel got herself under control, mentally yanking her inner wolf up by the scruff of the neck and subduing the snarling and frightened beast.

But, as soon as she did, her field of vision grayed, her focus wavering. She blinked rapidly, willing her contacts to help her see. If she passed out here, someone would surely summon paramedics. If they ran a blood test…

She couldn't let that happen. The law of the Pack forbade it.

Leaving her half-filled shopping cart in the middle of the aisle, she ran from the store in a blind panic.

Ignoring shouts to stop, she slid into her car and fumbled with the key. After two attempts, she finally got it in the ignition, started the car and peeled out of the parking lot as the sound of sirens drew closer.

Though her entire body shook so violently she could scarcely concentrate, she gripped the steering wheel and stared at the road. Adrenaline helped, as did her overwhelming determination to get home. Praying she wouldn't encounter a cop, she stomped on the accelerator and raced down the curving two-lane road. She only slowed a little as she made the right turn onto her street with her tires screeching.

Heart pounding, body shaking, she stomped on the brake to stop, sending gravel flying. She'd made it! Slamming the car into Park, she snatched the keys from the ignition and pushed open her door.

The ramshackle cabin—now her sanctuary—had never looked so inviting. Still shuddering, she tried to run, stumbling as if she were drugged. After falling once and skinning her knee and palm on the gravel, she continued on. Finally, she reached the doorstep.

Only when she was safely inside, door locked, did she allow herself to collapse on the couch, her breathing ragged, heartbeat erratic. A trickle of warmth made her glance at her knee and she saw she was bleeding.

Inside her, the wolf howled and snarled and began fighting again.

No! Jewel fought back, furious at her traitorous body. She wanted to change, had to change, but knew right now she couldn't, not without serious injury or worse. The wolf understood none of this, surging to be free.

Somehow, after a violent, inner battle, Jewel subdued her beast.

She'd won, again. But at what cost? If she didn't change soon, she'd die.

Exhausted, she clenched her hands into fists, ordering them to stop trembling. When that failed, she jumped to her feet. Though her legs shook and her body felt weak, she paced, trying to find a solution.

Again the urge to change rippled through her, stronger this time. Again, she struggled against herself. Pacing, growling low in her throat, she whined and snarled, cajoled and pleaded. Human words mingled with animal sounds and, using the last of her strength, again she fought and won.

But this was only the first part of the battle. Now came the sexual need, always a result of her aborted changes. Leo had delighted in this, purposely goading her to change, knowing whatever he'd done to her would make that impossible. He hadn't cared that she might die, nor had he given a damn what toll it would take on her body, on her mind.

Leo had found a perverse excitement, taking his pleasure and reveling in her weakness. When he'd finished, he'd left her to lick her wounds in humiliation, mortified that she had no control over her own body.

She could control the wolf, but she could not control her sexual hunger. Even now, alone, desire raged through her and she craved a man's touch, a man's hard body... Closing her eyes, she pictured Colton Reynolds, and the way he'd backed away from her need.

No. Forcibly, she pushed his image away, using her own hands to pleasure herself, frantic in her search for release. She was alone and must always be alone. Until she could repair the broken part of her, she had no choice.

Her climax came with a fury that sent her to her knees, moaning.

Spent and shaken, when it was over she stepped into the shower and let the hot water soothe her aching muscles. Clean and sore, finally Jewel dropped onto her bed and gave herself over to exhaustion. From experience she knew her sleep would be long and deep, and she'd awaken ravenous. Since she was pretty much out of food, except for a few eggs, a few slices of bread and an orange, that could be a problem, but it was one she couldn't solve.

* * *

There had been an incident at the grocery store. No less than three people called Colton to tell him. A woman had had some sort of fit or seizure and, while paramedics were en route, she'd recovered and run from the store.

This in itself, while a cause for great speculation in Anniversary, wasn't enough to excite Colton. But the woman's description matched Jewel Smith's.

His boss wanted him to investigate it for the paper. Remembering the incident by the lakeside, Colton wanted to make sure she was all right.

Snatching his car keys off his desk with one hand while closing his flip phone with the other, he hurried from the newspaper office and climbed in his Dodge Ram 1500 pickup.

He sped the two blocks to the Burrus Store, parked and hurried inside, where he met with the manager. An affable guy named Bubby, with the build and red face to match, he punctuated his conversation with enough swear words to make a sailor blush. Used to him, Colton never even flinched.

Despite his intention to remain detached, when Bubby began describing the woman, Colton's stomach again began to burn. He reached in his pocket for his ever-present roll of antacids, popped two and impatiently motioned to Bubby to finish.

Though he'd grabbed his notepad, Colton didn't bother to write anything down. Tall with long blond hair and shocking emerald eyes only described one woman in town. Jewel Smith.

"Do you think it was drugs?" Colton asked, hating the pity that flashed in the other guy's face at his question.

"Nah." Bubby shook his head, sending the sizeable wattle under his chin to wiggling. "Not everybody is using drugs, Colt. Just because your—"

"Then what was it?" Colton cut him off, well aware that most folks in Anniversary thought he carried his personal vendetta against drugs a bit too far. But then they'd never lost a child to drugs either.

With a shrug, Bubby indicated his lack of knowledge. "Don't know. Some kind of epileptic thing, maybe. My grandma used to—"

"Did you see what she was driving?"

Bubby hadn't, but several other witnesses had noticed the car.

"Beat-up old Buick," one man said, scratching his head. "No AC either. She drives with the windows down."

The description of the car clinched it. The woman was definitely Jewel.

"Thanks." Hurrying back outside, Colton climbed

in his truck and headed over toward the old Pryor place. He'd check things out for himself and make sure Jewel was all right. Hopefully, she wouldn't be wandering around outside naked or worse, unconscious and alone, waiting for someone to awaken her.

Again the mental image of the desire that had darkened her eyes before she'd kissed him, of her lithe body, impossibly long legs and high breasts. He cursed out loud, though there was no one to hear him, furious at his instant arousal.

Pulling into her gravel drive, he parked behind her car. Her engine was still making clicking sounds and the hood was hot, telling him she'd arrived home recently.

His light taps on her door went unanswered, so he hurried down to the shore, carefully combing the woods. When he found no sign of her there, his worry mounted. Irrational yes, but he kept remembering her unconscious on the ground. Telling himself he'd touch nothing, only make sure she was safe, he went to the back of the house, where he knew the window was shaky.

As he'd suspected, due to its condition, the locking mechanism was loose, and a few quick wiggles of the frame unlocked it. Telling himself this was a fantastic opportunity to do some good investigative reporting, he pushed open the bottom and climbed up inside. Knowing he'd be in the kitchen helped, and he jumped down from the countertop with relative ease.

Standing stock still, he listened. The only sound he heard was the soft ticking of a clock. The place smelled like citrus, as if she'd just finished peeling and eating a juicy orange. But he saw no sign anyone had dined on anything. The house appeared deserted.

Maybe, despite her car in the drive, Jewel wasn't home. But where could she have gone, especially if she was sick?

Heart thudding in his chest, he padded down the small hallway toward the single bedroom.

As soon as he entered the small room, he realized she was there, sleeping or unconscious. Staring, he also realized he was in big, big trouble as his body thickened.

Sprawled across the bed on top of the faded quilt, Jewel looked as beautiful and alluring as he remembered, maybe more so. Colton froze, unable to keep his gaze from drinking in the sight of her.

She was all right. He needed to go before she woke and saw him. He couldn't blame her then if she called the police.

Stumbling, he made it out without disturbing her. Once he reached his truck, he sat inside, shocked at what he'd done.

He felt like a stalker.

Dragging a shaky hand across his face, he wondered what the hell was wrong with him. The more distance he put between himself and this woman, the better. He knew it. Yet he couldn't seem to stay away.

Later, after a shower, he felt too restless to stay put. He needed a cold beer, or two or three. Pulling on a pair of jeans and boots, he headed to the highway and Jack's Grill on the Water, his favorite place to grab a cold beer and shoot a game of pool. They had pretty decent burgers, too.

Once there, he found a group of locals hanging around the bar listening to a woman wail into the microphone while guitars twanged.

Conversation eventually turned to the new— and beautiful—single woman, Jewel Smith. Of course. Even the fates were against him. Resigned, he listened rather than contributing to the talk.

"I've seen her somewhere," John Cassel muttered, staring into his beer bottle. "But I can't remember where."

The band started up again, drowning out what else John said, but Colton didn't care. He knew the feeling. Once he could put a finger on where he'd seen her, maybe he could stop thinking about her.

He'd even dragged himself out to this bar, a

place he used to come every week, though he'd stopped recently. But he needed a distraction, something to keep his mind on other things besides her. So far nothing, not even fishing, his favorite escape, had worked. Why not try noise and smoke, booze and inebriated, tanned women? What did he have to lose?

Christ. He rubbed his eyes. He'd already lost it all.

"What's wrong?" Rick Bantam, newly elected mayor, punched Colton's arm. "You look like someone died."

"Nothing like that." Despite his lighthearted tone, Colton's insides clenched. Rick couldn't know how his careless words stabbed him. After all, it had been two years. Normal people recovered in two years, right?

But then, Colton had never claimed to be normal.

"He's just trying to remember where he's seen Jewel Smith. We both think she looks familiar." John tapped his foot in time to the music. His easy grin said he didn't really care.

"You don't remember her?" Rick's bushy gray brows rose. "It's only been six months since she was on the news."

Colton sat up, carefully placing his beer bottle on the bar. "On the news? Are you telling me you know who she is?"

"Sure, man." Rick leaned close, lowering his voice. "Though I'm willing to bet she doesn't want anyone else to know. I'm surprised you didn't place her, as obsessed as you are with stopping drugs."

So his suspicions *were* on target.

Suppressing the urge to grab the other man by the shirt, Colton waited. If he tried for nonchalance, he knew he'd fail, so he said nothing.

Neither did Rick. He sipped his beer while leisurely surveying the packed room.

Seconds ticked into minutes. Finally, Colton couldn't take it anymore. "Who is she?"

Rick's mild brown gaze met his. "Sorry. Despite the blond hair, Jewel Smith is a dead ringer for Julie Licciardoni, former wife of Leo Licciardoni. Don't tell me you've forgotten about his trial."

Colton hadn't forgotten. How could he? The indictment, arrest and trial had been sensationalized in every media outlet, including his former employer's.

"If I remember right, she entered the Witness Protection Program," Rick continued. "That must be why she's here, with a different name and hair color."

"Excuse me." Draining the last of his beer, Colton set the empty bottle down. "I've got to go." Without waiting for Rick's response, he pushed his way through the crowd toward the exit. Smoke curled around him, curdling his gut, stinging his eyes.

Once outside, he took great gulps of the humid air.

"Are you all right?" John had followed him out. "You don't look so good."

"I'm fine." Colton waved his friend away, summoning what he hoped vaguely resembled a smile. "Stomach's messed up. Must be something I ate earlier."

John nodded, mumbling something about women as he turned to go back in the bar.

Colton barely noticed. He started the truck and turned left on Samsun Road, heading home. He'd been wrong about Jewel Smith, née Julie Licciardoni, in a big way.

She'd been the prosecution's chief witness against her husband's cartel, testifying against her own husband, while simultaneously filing for divorce. She'd claimed she hadn't known about her husband's illegal activities and, when she'd learned of them, she'd turned the man in.

It was entirely possible, he thought with a shake of his head, that Jewel was one other person who hated drugs as much as him.

But then what explained the way he'd found her, naked and unconscious, acting as if she was high? Could the perfect witness have lied? Was

she perhaps a user, a victim of the very same
designer drugs her husband's people had peddled?

He didn't know, but he had to find out.

Chapter 4

Jewel paced, wishing she hadn't needed to abort her earlier attempt at grocery shopping. She had to feed both herself and the beast within. She needed food, but worse, she needed iron. Red meat, preferably a T-bone steak, cooked rare. Her mouth watered at the thought.

Inside her, the caged wolf snarled.

They were both ravenous. Empty stomach clenched in knots, she snatched up her car keys. She had no choice but to make the attempt again.

"Behave," she chastised herself, praying the wolf would remain contained.

Outside, the humid air caressed her skin. She walked to her car, clenching her teeth to keep them from chattering. Not from cold, but because the effort to control the change was becoming more and more difficult.

She didn't know how much longer she could continue without making another attempt. She didn't know if the next attempt would be her last.

One problem at a time. For now, she needed to focus on food. On survival.

This time, she chose a different market. This one was larger, newer, more anonymous. Finding a slot near the door, she parked. Taking a deep breath, she exited her vehicle and walked into the brightly lit store, grabbing a shiny metal cart.

So far, so good.

She stormed up one aisle and down the next. Grabbing items off the shelves and tossing them in her cart as quickly as she could, she made it through the entire store without incident. The checkout process went smoothly, though Jewel knew better than to relax. When she let her guard down too much, the wolf would seek an opening, a way out.

Declining the teenager's offer to help load the bags into her car, Jewel hit the parking lot at a jog then unloaded the cart into her trunk. She hurried through that process, too. The sooner she got home, the better off they'd all be.

One thing about this old heap, she thought, the trunk could fit a ton of stuff. Or one dead body, she thought ruefully, slamming the trunk and thinking again of Leo.

She even returned the shopping cart to the cart collection area before she left. Confidence soaring, she did a mental victory dance as she climbed into her car.

Driving back to the rental house, she began to finally relax. She had her food, there'd been no episode of changing, and after she got everything unloaded and put up, she'd cook a big steak dinner.

Coasting up to the first stop sign, she applied her brakes.

There were none.

The pedal went all the way to the floor.

A huge eighteen-wheeler had almost reached the intersection. And this wasn't a four-way stop.

Lips drawn back in a grimace, she fought for her life. Jerking the steering wheel to the right, she attempted to avoid the intersection. The rear end fishtailed. The car was too heavy. Despite her attempt to turn it, sheer forward momentum kept her continuing toward the intersection.

The semi driver lay on his horn. Loaded, he brought about eighty thousand pounds bearing down on her car. His tires squealed as he tried to brake.

Damn it! Manually shifting from drive into second, she attempted to slow the Buick. The engine screamed and the car jerked.

Not enough. Not enough.

The huge grill of the Peterbilt loomed.

Impact.

Rear passenger side. The car caved in. Her seat belt held, though her chin hit the steering wheel.

Slow motion. She tasted blood. Her own.

So this is what it's like to die.

She saw it all, her world tilting like some distorted carnival mirror. Her last seconds were full of images and sounds—shattering glass, the scream of the air brakes as the truck driver tried to stop. Metal on metal, her car crushing like an empty tin can under a giant foot.

Jewel screamed again and again. The sound became a howl.

The truck finally shuddered to a stop, her car impaled on its front.

She couldn't see, couldn't breathe, couldn't feel.

Then, the wolf erupted in panic, fighting for freedom now, fiercely struggling to shed the human form. The flight instinct, the need for survival, overrode all else.

She wanted to live.

Jewel did, too. She fought the change, knowing she'd never survive if the wolf broke free.

Colton received the call on his way to the boathouse, just after stopping at the bait shop for a fresh crop of minnows. "There's been a horrible accident on Harbor Road." Sue Kearney, one of the police-department dispatchers, liked to keep him informed. "I thought you might like to know."

Even a minor accident was news in a town like Anniversary. If the week had been especially slow, the paper might even put the story on the front page.

"Thanks, Sue. I'll head over that way right now." Clicking the phone shut, Colton pulled into the first driveway he came to and reversed the car. He'd hoped to get in a few hours of mid-afternoon fishing, but the minnows would keep. Duty called.

He made it to the accident scene in less than five minutes, coasting to a stop and parking on the side of the road. He grabbed his camera and, pushing past the yellow tape, waved at the sheriff as he made his way to view the wreckage. The jack-knifed semi loomed like a giant, the shaken truck driver huddled by himself, talking on his cell phone. Groceries were scattered all over the highway and roadside.

After snapping several pictures, he took a look at the other vehicle. Colton's heart stopped. Mangled and barely recognizable, it looked like Jewel's—or Julie's—car. The twisted and crumpled pieces of metal told him it would be a miracle if anyone had survived.

"No one could live through that." He heard his own voice from a distance, as he forced his shaky legs to move. Circling the wreckage, he snapped photo after photo. He saw no sign of a body, though blood darkened the steering wheel and the remains of the front seat.

Sheriff Tucker came over. "Surprisingly, someone did, even though this car was too old to have an air bag."

Colton could barely speak. "Where..." Clearing his throat, he tried again. "Where is she?"

"She's been transported by ambulance into Athens. I'm thinking they may have to use Care Flight to send out to Parkland Hospital in Dallas."

"Who..." Taking a deep breath, Colton swallowed. Though he suspected he knew the answer, he had to ask. "Who was it?"

"I can't think of her name." Tucker scratched

the back of his neck. "Ah, hell. It was that new woman, you know, the one that lives out at the old Pryor place. Name starts with a *J* or an *L,* I believe. You know her, don't you?"

Mouth dry, he nodded. "Jewel. Jewel Smith."

Snapping his fingers, Tucker nodded. "That's her. She was unconscious when the ambulance loaded her up. Her injuries are pretty severe."

Jewel.

Surprised to realize his hands were shaking, Colton walked over to the trucker, who'd just closed his phone and looked lost. "What happened?"

Eyes wild, the other man was barely coherent. "I hope I didn't kill her, man, but it wasn't my fault. She had a stop sign, but she didn't stop." He pointed to a set of black skid marks on the pavement. "It looked like she tried to at the last minute."

"I'm surprised she's still alive." Having followed Colton over, Sheriff Tucker clapped a hand on his shoulder. "Matter of fact, if you want to get more on the story for the paper, you'd better hurry to the hospital."

As a reporter, he didn't usually interview the accident victim until they were out of ICU. As a man, however… Heart pounding, Colton took off, starting his pickup and peeling out.

Athens was a good thirty minutes away, if one

drove the speed limit. He made it there in twenty, blowing through the hospital doors at a dead run.

The plump nurse manning the admitting desk told him Ms. Smith was in intensive care. Since he wasn't immediate family, he wasn't allowed to visit. She pointed the way to the small waiting room.

Frustrated, he paced the halls instead. What had made her do such a thing? The truck driver had said she'd run the stop sign. Had she been using, or had she experienced another one of her seizures?

Until he talked to her, he wouldn't know.

If he talked to her.

For the first time since his daughter had died, Colton Reynolds found himself uttering a prayer.

She couldn't let them take her blood. Fighting back to consciousness, she noted first the absence of her wolf-self. Stunned into retreat by injury and shock, that was one less thing she'd have to deal with.

First, she had to get out of this hospital. Though the medical staff might see her injuries as severe, she knew her supercharged immune system would repair the damage quickly.

One of the primary Pack rules was avoiding discovery by humans. If she truly needed medical care, she'd have to find a Pack doctor. Since she was in the middle of nowhere, Texas, she had no idea how to even contact the Pack, nor did she want to.

She knew if she did, Leo would find her. He had friends and flunkies in a lot of different Packs, coast to coast. Most of all, she wanted to stay alive.

Blinking her eyes into focus, she tried to concentrate past the throbbing headache. The first thing she needed to do was take stock of her injuries. The hospital staff had done a good job of cleaning her up, washing the blood from her and getting her into a hospital gown. Her left leg was bandaged, and she had another large bandage on her side.

Was anything broken? She moved her fingers, then her hands, relieved when she felt no pain. All of her right toes wiggled on command, but trying to move her left brought excruciating pain.

Okay. Something *was* broken. From past experience, she knew her bones would reknit and heal much faster than a human's. She couldn't let them put a cast on her or worse, attempt surgery.

She had to get out of here before they found out what she was. At least she could still see. She hadn't lost her contacts and the hospital hadn't removed them.

"You're awake." A woman's voice, sounding pleased. "Good. Just in time. We need to try again to take your blood. We're having trouble identifying your blood type. Something must be wrong with the machine."

Oh, no. This, she couldn't allow. If they figured out her blood was an anomaly, she'd be in trouble.

"Stop," she croaked, pushing at the nurse bearing down on her with a large syringe. "I don't want that."

Even if she was completely paranoid, better safe than sorry.

"It won't hurt." The large woman kept coming. Panicked, Jewel pushed at her, shoving her away and into the wall and sending the syringe clattering to the ground. She'd used too much force. Sometimes she forgot her own strength.

"I'm sorry." Apologizing as she moved, Jewel placed her left leg gingerly on the floor, using her right to balance most of her weight. "I've got to go."

Wide-eyed, the nurse stared at her. "You can't. You may not realize it, but you were badly hurt."

"I'm better." Hobbling toward the hall, Jewel just reached the door when the woman lunged for a button on the machine by the bed. Immediately, an alarm sounded.

Crap. Jewel kept going, trying to hold her hospital gown in place with one hand. Though she had no idea where to go, or even how to get there, she knew beyond a doubt she had to flee.

Rounding the corner, she collided with a man.

"Sorry," she mumbled, stumbling back. A shock of recognition went through her as she realized the man was Colton Reynolds, the newspaper reporter. For a second she wondered what he was doing there, then decided she didn't care. Maybe he'd be an ally.

"Jewel!" His gaze searched her face. "Are you all right?"

"Please." She grabbed his arm. "Help me. I've got to get out of here."

He opened his mouth to speak, but before he could, two orderlies, a nurse and a man in a white coat who could only be a doctor converged on them.

"You need to come with me." The doctor took her arm, giving the orderlies a meaningful look.

Panicked, Jewel shook off his hand. "I'm leaving."

"No, you're not." At the doctor's gesture, the two orderlies moved in, flanking her on each side. "You need to get back in that bed and let us examine you."

"Just a minute." The calm voice of reason, Colton moved to intercept. "If she wants to go, you have to let her. You can't force someone into the hospital."

"Who are you?" The doctor looked down his nose.

"A friend," he said firmly. "And if Ms. Smith says she wants to leave, then she's leaving."

"This woman was in a serious accident. She

was brought in by ambulance. She shouldn't even be conscious, much less standing."

As Jewel opened her mouth to speak, Colton touched her arm, forestalling her. "Perhaps she appeared to be hurt worse than she actually is."

"Not according to the X-rays."

"Please," Jewel whimpered, fighting back the panic. Her wolf side had now awakened and was urging her to flee.

Something in her expression must have decided him. "Sorry, doc." Colton took her arm. "She's going with me. I'll bring her back if she needs any other medical care."

"There's paperwork," the nurse warned, brandishing a clipboard like a weapon. "She can't leave without signing the release forms."

"I'm not signing them," the doctor warned.

"If he's not, then I'm not." With that, Jewel walked away, shaking her leg to iron out the kinks. She knew her limp was already less noticeable and that they'd wonder, but she didn't care.

Colton hurried after her, catching her arm once they'd reached the parking lot. "Wait."

"I'm not going back in there," she warned. "What are you doing here anyway?"

"I'm a reporter, remember? I got called to the accident scene. When I saw the wreck and realized it was you, I came out here to make sure you were all right." He searched her face. "They said you were badly injured."

"They were wrong. I'm fine."

"You don't seem to be all that hurt," he agreed. "Though I don't see how that's possible, considering the shape of your car."

Her car. Jewel's spirits sank. Now she was without transportation. Buying another vehicle would use up a lot of her precious stash of money. "I'm going home," she said, moving forward.

Again, he kept pace with her. "I don't blame you. But your place is a five-mile walk or more and you're in a hospital gown. Would you like a ride?"

She hesitated, eyeing him sideways. His relaxed expression gave away nothing. "I would," she said finally, pulling away. "If you're sure you don't mind."

He pointed to his pickup, punching the key fob to unlock the doors. "Hop in and we'll go."

Once she'd buckled herself in, he started the engine and they pulled out of the hospital parking lot. He was surprised no one had followed them. But then, he'd never seen anyone refuse treatment before.

"Are you all right?" Colton asked, keeping his tone nonconfrontational.

"Yes." She leaned back in the seat while he drove.

To his shock, he realized she was shivering. "Are you cold?"

"No. When I had the accident, I was on my way home from the grocery store with a trunk load of groceries. Now, I realize my foray for food was all for nothing. I need to eat."

He nodded. "I'll run through the drive-through at Burger Barn. Tell me what happened?"

"My brakes failed." Her flat voice told him she thought it was something more. "I pushed the brake pedal and it went all the way to the floor." She took a deep breath and met his gaze squarely. "I think they were tampered with."

Because of who she was, he realized he had to take her seriously. But first, should he let her know her secret was out?

If he'd recognized her, so would others.

The Burger Barn was up ahead, on the right.

"Tampered with?" Stalling for time, he scratched his chin, a nervous habit he'd never been able to shake. "Why would someone do that?"

Staring out the window, she didn't answer.

He signaled a right turn and pulled into the drive-through. "What do you want?"

"Three hamburgers, cooked medium rare. Diet Coke."

"The mini-burgers?"

"No, the doubles."

"The doubles?"

"I told you, I'm starving." The look she gave him dared him to argue.

"Fine. I'm having the chicken-fried steak sandwich."

"Steak?" She perked up at that. "That sounds good. Order me one of those, too."

"Too? In place of one of the burgers?"

"No, in addition to."

He placed the order, paid and pulled forward to the second window. Only once he'd accepted the grease-spotted bags and pulled away did he decide he needed a better plan.

"Let's go by my place and eat," he said, watching as she dropped the burger she'd been about to unwrap back into the sack. "You can borrow one of my shirts."

"I'd rather you drop me off at home."

This time, he didn't answer.

When they turned into his drive, she made a sound, low in her throat. "It's...beautiful."

"Thanks." He'd wanted to see her reaction, knowing how he'd felt the first time he'd seen the house. Set back among the pines and oaks, the weathered cedar house looked as if it would have been equally at home in remote Alaska. Floor-to-ceiling windows and several skylights completed the natural look, giving a feeling of openness.

He loved the place.

Grabbing one of his T-shirts and a pair of old, soft cotton shorts, he took them to Jewel. Shaking her head, she grabbed them, disappearing into the bathroom to change.

When she returned, she visibly inhaled the aroma of burgers and fries, eyeing the sack with an intent look on her face.

Handing her one of the sacks, he led the way into the kitchen. She went straight for the table, upending the bag and casting him an apologetic look as she ripped into a handful of fries.

He waited until she'd finished her third burger, barely chewing. He couldn't help but watch, astonished as she scarfed down the meal as though she were starving.

"How long has it been since you ate?"

Regarding him warily, she lifted one shoulder in a shrug. "I don't know."

"Days?"

"Why?"

Because he'd slipped back into reporter mode. Because he was making small talk until he told her the truth. Since he couldn't say any of that, he went for the most logical explanation.

"Your health. You've passed out at least once that I know of, and you had the episode in the grocery store."

"You know about that?"

He crossed his arms. "Everyone knows about that. Anniversary's a small town."

"I'm okay," she said. Her uncertain tone let them both know she was lying.

Since he could think of no easy way to break the bad news, he waited until she'd finished polishing off the last of his French fries. "I know who you are."

She froze. The haunted look in her huge green eyes was replaced by a flash of terror. "What do you mean?"

"I kept thinking you looked familiar, like a celebrity or someone who'd been in the news. One of the guys also recognized you and reminded me of where I'd seen you."

"But I changed my hair, my name..." Her entire body had gone on instant alert, radiating tension. The bruise on her cheek had faded, too rapidly to be normal.

"You look too unusual to be able to hide." He put it as gently as he could. "Your features are instantly recognizable."

She stood. "I have to leave."

"Wait." Jumping to his feet, he reached out to

stop her. "Tell me what you're running from. Maybe I can help."

To his shock, she cringed away from his hand. "Don't touch me!"

"Fine. But why are you running? Your ex-husband's in prison."

"That shows how little you really know." Her laugh was bitter, containing not one trace of humor. "Leo may be locked up, but his network extends all across the country."

"He swore to have you killed."

"Yes. And Leo means what he says. Even now, they're hunting me."

"Did you enter the Witness Protection Program? Is that why you're here in Anniversary?"

"No." Her bleak look told him how little she trusted anyone, including him. "The risk was too great. Leo had guys on the inside, for all I know. I cut my losses and ran."

"You're on your own?" He could scarcely believe her courage, both then and now.

"Yes." Swallowing, she twisted her hands together in front of her. "And I'm not…well."

Something twisted inside him, a tug at the place in his chest that housed his atrophied heart. "Not well," he repeated. "I hate to pry, but is it terminal?"

"It could be, but I'm hoping to get better." Since he was blocking the doorway, she went to the window instead, turning the heavy oak blinds to peer outside. When she turned again to face him, her expression was resigned. "What do you want?"

"I'm not sure I follow."

"You. Obviously you want something from me."

He thought for a moment, pushing away the thoughts of hot, wild sex. "No."

"Then why tell me this?"

"I thought you should know. For your own protection."

"I see." But he knew she didn't, not really. "I'd better be going."

At her words, he knew without a doubt she didn't just mean going back to her rented cabin. "You're leaving town?"

A flicker of surprise in her eyes, then she nodded. "I don't have a choice. If you and this other man recognized me, so will others. It won't be long before word gets back to Leo, if it hasn't already."

"New York is a long way from east Texas."

"Not far enough, apparently." She sighed. "Maybe that's why my brakes failed. Maybe he's already found me."

Though he could identify with her paranoia—he'd been paranoid, too, right after Angela had died and he'd learned his wife had been dealing drugs behind his back—he realized with a mild sense of shock that he didn't want her to go.

"Let me help you," he heard himself say. "I think you could use a friend."

Stone-faced, she regarded him. "Why would you want to do that? You barely know me."

"Why?" How could he explain to her what he didn't know himself. "My daughter died because of drugs."

"So I heard. Men like Leo distribute them, all around the country. He got rich from people like your daughter."

"You helped put him away."

"Yes."

"And you left it all behind. The money, the mansions and fancy cars, all of it."

"Yes."

Now he moved to touch her arm, and this time she didn't flinch. "That's why I want to help you. Please, let me."

Chapter 5

At the police impound lot a day later, checking out her ruined car, Colton swore. "You were right." He stood, dusting his hands off on his jeans. "The brake line was split."

"Split? You mean cut, don't you? Damn it." She paced, the wind catching strands of her hair. "He's found me."

Colton wanted to touch her. Instead, he crammed his hands into his pockets. "Don't jump to conclusions. We need to check with the police. The first thing they always do in situations like this is check for brake fluid. It would have squirted out when you went to apply the brakes."

She folded her arms. "Tell me the truth. Does it look like it's been cut?"

Reluctantly, he nodded. "Yes."

"Let me look." She dropped to the ground, peering under the twisted wreckage. "Show me what to look for."

He showed her the left front brake line, the only one that had been cut. The right side was still intact.

"That would be enough to make my brakes fail?" she asked. "They wouldn't have to cut both of them?"

"No." He got to his feet. "Let me make a call to the police station. I'm sure they saw this, too."

"Then why wouldn't they tell me?" Her eyes widened. "You don't think one of them…"

"Come on, Jewel. You can't be suspecting everyone. You'll make yourself a nervous wreck."

"I know." Sighing, she lifted her face to the sun and sniffed. "I can't even get a scent."

"Get a…" He frowned. "What do you mean?"

Her startled look told him she hadn't meant to speak out loud. "Nothing. Never mind." She got to her feet, her expression heavy. "I guess what happened doesn't matter. Either way, it's time for me to move on."

"Move on?" She'd startled him. "Why? You don't know for sure he's found you."

"Why else would my brake line be cut? Come on, I'd rather be safe than sorry. Especially where he's concerned. You don't know Leo. When he says he's going to do something, he won't rest until it's done."

Since her ex-husband had very publicly sworn to see her dead, Colton could understand her paranoia. Still, though he hated to admit it, he didn't want to see her go.

"Let's think this through. The man's in prison. If this really *is* him, how's he finding you?"

Her troubled gaze touched on his face before skittering away. "He has his ways."

"Not a good enough answer. Did you contact anyone back where you used to live?"

She shook her head. "I have no one back there. Both my adoptive parents are dead."

"What about friends?"

"Leo made sure I had no friends."

The way she spoke of what must have been complete and utter isolation touched him. How lonely she must have been.

He forced his mind back to the subject at hand. "Have you used a credit card or a cell phone?"

"No. No credit cards and I threw away the cell phone Leo'd given me. I brought a prepaid one with cash, under my new name. There's no way he could trace me with that."

"What made you choose Jewel Smith?"

A faint flush colored her cheeks, though she lifted her chin and squarely met his gaze. "Because I think of myself as emerging from under the ground. Someday, I'll shine again. Though I'm no diamond," she added.

"No, not a diamond," he said softly, unable to help himself. "More like an opal, mysterious and quiet, until you turn it the right way and it flashes fire."

She laughed and he could tell she was pleased.

"Where will you go this time?" he asked, when he really wanted to know if she had someone, somewhere, to help protect her.

She shrugged. "I'm not sure. Maybe north, into Canada. I've heard British Columbia is beautiful."

His chest felt tight. She might as well have said Australia. There was no way he could keep an eye out for her so far away. Why he even wanted to, he couldn't explain, even to himself.

Crossing his arms and watching her, he shook his head. "You'll run again, find a place, settle, and make a home. Until the next accident happens. And then what?"

"This was no accident. Come on, Colton. How

many people do you know who've had their brake line magically snap on them?"

She had a point, but he wanted to make a point of his own. "Hear me out. Are you going to spend the rest of your life running?"

"I don't know."

"I do. Every time you think he's tracked you down, you'll go. What kind of life will you have, always looking over your shoulder?"

Her expression turned hard. "Why do you care?"

"Damned if I know." He turned, thought about walking away and realized he couldn't do it. "But, for some odd reason, I do."

She stared at him. From her silence he could tell he'd surprised her.

Ah, damn. He'd even surprised himself.

"What are you suggesting?" she asked.

He stayed silent, afraid to open his mouth, afraid he'd say the wrong thing.

"So I run. And I live. If I don't, I die. What choice do I have?"

He ran a hand through his hair. "There's got to be another option."

"Really? Then tell me what. Give me some suggestions." Her eyes had gone dark, the color of the lake in a storm. "Maybe I should hunt this guy down, find out who he is and stop him."

He started to chuckle, before realizing she wasn't joking. "You're serious."

"Yes." Now she came closer, lifting her gaze to his. "Even if I stay on the run, I want to be prepared for an attack. Why do you think I signed up for the self-defense class?"

"An excellent idea."

"Maybe. But not against cut brake lines and bullets. If the car had exploded, I'd have been killed."

She was right, though looking at her, he couldn't even tell she'd been in an accident only yesterday. All of her bruises had completely disappeared.

"I'm thinking about buying a gun," she said.

Now she'd shocked him. "A gun. Do you know how to use it?"

"No, but there are classes I can take, right?"

He nodded. "In Texas, you can get a license to carry a concealed weapon once you've completed the course."

She moved even closer, so close he could smell the light, musky scent of her. "Do you have this license?"

Barely able to concentrate, he tore his gaze away from her lips. "Yes."

"Then you know how to shoot."

Too late, he saw where this was going. "I do,"

he said reluctantly. "I use target practice to relieve my tension."

"Teach me," she breathed, her breath tickling his chin. "Please, Colton. If I stay, you've got to help me."

Now he was confused. "You're staying?"

"Maybe. For a little while. If you help me."

"Earlier, you said you were ill. What's wrong with you?"

"I am ill." The expectant look vanished from her face. "Just not in the way you think."

Colton shook his head. "If I'm going to help you, I need you to be honest with me."

"Not about this. There are some things you're better off not knowing."

His chest clenched. For a moment, he couldn't breathe. His ex-wife, Paula, had thought that way, too, hiding both her own addiction and that of their teenage daughter. Never again.

He took a deep breath. "When you say that, I think of one thing. Drug addiction."

She stared, her green eyes wide and guileless, but her expression pinched and worried. He waited for her to speak, hoping she'd tell him he was wrong.

When she didn't, he lifted his hand. "I'm out of here. You do whatever you want."

"Colton—"

One last chance, damn her. He'd give her one last chance. "Are you addicted to some kind of drugs?"

"No. Not even close." Unsmiling, she met his gaze to let him know that this at least, wasn't the secret she was hiding. "Not even Leo could force me to do that. And believe me, he tried."

"He tried?" This was incomprehensible. "Why? Why would anyone do that?"

"You don't know Leo." She sighed. "He wanted me totally compliant, his own personal slave." She shuddered, lost in the horror of her own memories.

Feeling as if he were tumbling down a particularly steep hill, Colton touched her—how could he not? He put his arms around her and drew her close. She tucked her head under his chin, her initial stiffness giving way slowly.

For a moment, he simply held her, knowing she could hear the thudding of his heart. Finally, he asked the question he'd never understood, even before he'd known this woman, when he'd watched her husband's trial on TV. "Why'd you marry someone like him, Jewel?"

"I didn't know."

Three simple words, yet his imagination ran with them. He knew from personal experience how easily someone you loved could hide their true nature.

"I—" she began.

"Shhh." Keeping his arms around her, he tried not to let the feel of her full breasts affect him, or the curve of her waist and intoxicating scent arouse him. "Tell me about your illness."

At his request, she stiffened and moved away.

"I can't." The flatness of her tone came not from fear, but something else. "It has nothing to do with drugs. That'll have to be enough for you."

Again, the reporter in him was intrigued. The man in him wanted her back in his arms. "Jewel…" he started.

"I'd like to go home," she interrupted, her expression fierce and determined. Only the slight catch in her voice revealed her inner emotions. "I can't think, and I need to clear my head."

"You won't tell me." This wasn't a question.

Regardless, she answered "No."

He fished his keys from his pocket, jingling them. "Then you're right. It's time for you to go."

"Let me get one thing out of my glove box." Without waiting for a response, she went to her wrecked car, leaned in the busted-out passenger window and retrieved a box.

Silent, they both got in his truck and buckled their seat belts. He started the motor, debated questioning her again, and decided against it.

While he drove, he told himself this was for the

better. He'd drop her off at her place and from then on, leave her alone.

He didn't want a woman with secrets. Hell, he didn't want a woman at all, especially this woman, with her own brand of trouble.

As he drove, aching to touch her, he wondered when he'd started lying to himself.

Unsmiling, Jewel watched Colton's truck disappear around the corner, staring after him until long after he was gone.

Dragging herself to her front door, she let herself in and, once inside, began to pace. It was a good thing she'd sent Colton packing. Well-fed and restless, the wolf within lunged, tearing at her fragile control. She wanted out of the human-body cage.

Jewel knew it was time. She would have to attempt to change once more, even if the results were disastrous.

If only she had someone, another shifter, with her to help in case she failed. But, even back in New York, Leo had kept her isolated from the other women, claiming at first she was ill. Eventually, even her old friends had given up. For the entire five years of her marriage, she'd not been allowed a single female friend.

The one time she'd tried, Leo'd beaten her to within an inch of her life. She'd been lucky shifters healed fast. No one seeing her then would have questioned Leo's story that she was seriously ill.

After that, she hadn't tried again. She'd learned how to live alone, relying on herself. A Pack member who truly wasn't permitted to be part of the Pack. Leo'd even left a guard watching her. After each visitor had been turned away time and time again, people had stopped trying.

She ought to be used to being alone, but God how she wanted a friend. That was why she'd toyed with the idea of telling Colton. Luckily, she'd come to her senses before she had. Foolishness like that could get her killed.

No, she was better off alone.

Still, she couldn't help but wonder how Colton would have reacted. He already half believed her a druggie—what would he think if she started babbling about being a werewolf?

The wolf within howled, making her shiver.

Once, she'd thought a wolf's howl one of the loveliest sounds of nature. Now, the cry of the wolf within pointed out the bleakness of her current existence.

A shifter who couldn't change. Worse than the

constant fear, the inability to change chipped at the core of her being.

Of course she had to try again. She was a shifter, part wolf. Whatever Leo had done to her, given her, had to be wearing off by now. Had to be.

Time to set her wolf free.

Though the sun blazed high overhead, she stepped outside. The heat of the day hit her like an open oven, the humidity making it difficult to breathe. She walked to the edge of her lawn, enjoying the feel of the sun on her skin, dipping her toe into the tepid lake waters.

Moving into the slightly cooler shadows of the trees, Jewel took a deep breath, holding back the wolf with her last bit of strength.

Though her sundress would be ruined if she succeeded, she left it on, not wanting to be found naked and unconscious by some other man. Fingering her wolf necklace for luck, she muttered a quick prayer. She prayed this time the change would overcome her. That this time she'd be free to run and hunt as her lupine self.

Then, tears streaming down her cheeks, she crouched close to the ground, inhaling the moist scent of earth. Reaching deep within herself, she touched her wolf, awakening her sleeping other-self. Then, giving herself over to the change, she released the beast.

No matter where he went, Colton couldn't escape Jewel. The entire town was talking about the accident and her subsequent self-discharge from the hospital.

Colton had already finished his piece for the paper and turned it in. Like any good reporter, he'd stuck to the facts, merely mentioning that Jewel's injuries didn't appear to be as severe as first believed.

Or as severe as the X-rays had indicated, according to the doctor. Colton had gone back to interview him after he'd left Jewel. "Something had to be wrong with your machine."

"Maybe," the doctor admitted. "But I don't see how. Even if her bones weren't broken, which they were, she had internal injuries. She shouldn't have even been conscious, never mind walking."

None of this made any sense.

"She mentioned she was ill." Pen poised over paper, Colton watched the other man intently. "Do you happen to know what's wrong with her?"

"Ill?" For the first time, Dr. Wilson appeared to realize who Colton was—or wasn't. Pushing his glasses up his sharp nose, he glared. "I thought you were her husband or a family member. After all, you did help her leave the hospital."

"No, I'm just a friend."

The other man eyed his pad. "Are you a reporter?"

"Yes. For *The Anniversary Beacon.*"

"I see." Shoulders sagging, Dr. Wilson shook his head. "Unfortunately, privacy laws prevent me from commenting further." White coat flapping, the doctor hurried away, clearly already regretting what little he'd revealed.

So Colton had written his story, turned it in, and told himself he was done worrying about Jewel. He'd gone to Timberwolf's Pub to eat and watch the sun set over the lake.

For the first twenty minutes or so, he'd enjoyed the peace and quiet of the relatively deserted bar. But as the day began to wind down, the place filled up. First one guy, then another stopped by his table to say hello. Now, while trying to eat a bacon cheeseburger for his supper and chasing this monument to clogged arteries with an ice-cold beer, it seemed every guy in the bar wanted to talk about her. Jewel Smith. Colton couldn't chew and swallow fast enough even to pretend not to know anything.

Finally, he gave up and put the burger down. He hadn't been able to taste it anyway. He paid his check and decided to head out, get in his boat and do a little fishing. There, he'd find peace and quiet.

And in this at least, he was right. He used his trolling motor to make the boat go slowly, watching as the fiery sun headed gracefully closer to the horizon, and let his lines trail out after him.

He told himself he'd stay away from Jewel's place, and as dusk began to settle over the water, he kept good on his promise. But the wind blew from the south and pushed him toward her cove and he finally told himself he'd fish that part of the lake, but stay out of the cove water.

So he trolled back and forth, down the channels, avoiding the one turn that would take him near her place.

Then, he smelled smoke.

Someone burning leaves, no doubt, though the middle of summer was the wrong time of the year for that. No, this was wood smoke, making him think of chimneys and fireplaces. In ninety-eight-degree heat?

Standing up in his boat, he shaded his eyes with his hand. There, a thick plume of smoke. From one of the coves near the Pryor place.

There was nothing there to burn—except the Pryor place.

Jewel!

Starting the motor, he opened the throttle to full and took off across the lake.

As soon as he reached the cove, he realized his fears were well founded. Flames licked the roof of Jewel's rental house. He punched 911 on his cell, spoke briefly to the operator, then closed the phone, steering into the cove.

Ramming the boat ashore, he tossed the anchor on land, jumped on it hard as he passed and took off up the embankment. Where was she? Had she gotten out?

The front door was locked, though he knew the frame was rickety. With no time to waste climbing in a window, he rammed the door with his shoulder. As he'd known it would, the dry wood splintered.

Instantly, a thick cloud of smoke billowed out, blinding him.

"Jewel!" he shouted her name. The fire was still confined to the back area, her kitchen and extra bedroom, though it wouldn't be long before the entire house went up like the kindling it was.

Though the smoke threatened to blind him, he saw no sign of Jewel in the main room. He could only pray she hadn't been in the kitchen.

Crouching low to the ground, he ran for the

front bedroom. Jewel lay crumpled on the floor, unconscious.

Shouting her name again, he lifted her and, coughing and gasping for air, sprinted for the front door.

Outside, he collapsed on the ground, cushioning her with his body. As he reached to feel for a pulse, her chest heaved and she began coughing.

Behind them, the fire roared through the small frame house, engulfing it.

"Jewel." He lifted her up, raising her chin to help her breathe. "Wake up."

Slowly, her eyes opened, the vivid green clouded.

"Colton?" she murmured.

"Yeah." He started to tell her that her house was on fire, but before he could, she murmured something unintelligible and kissed him.

Too shocked to react at first, he kissed her back. Then, realizing what was happening, he pushed her away, holding her at arm's length while she struggled. For the first time he saw that her dress was ripped, as though she'd slashed at the material with a sharp knife. "What are you doing? What the hell's wrong with you?"

At his words, she went still, though desire still darkened her cloudy gaze. "I tried to—" She swallowed, her tone miserable. "When I try to change and fail, this is what happens. All that energy channels into a craving for sex."

Her words made no sense. Putting them down to a possible injury, he ignored his body's stirring and studied her. "You sound…confused. Are you all right? Are you hurt?"

"That noise…is there a…fire?" Narrowing her eyes, she sniffed. "I smell smoke." Before he could answer, she turned, gasping when she saw the flames consuming the old frame house. "My purse is in there. My wallet—all my money!" Gaze panicked, she climbed to her knees, as though she were considering attempting a mad dash to retrieve something that was no longer there.

"They're gone," he told her quietly. "I'm sorry."

Expression miserable, she jerked her head in a nod of sorts. "Did you call the fire department?"

"I called 911. They're on their way. Our department is volunteer, so it takes them a little longer to round up the people."

Glumly, she watched the fire crackle and dance. "By the time they get here, that house and everything inside will be ashes."

As if on cue, sirens sounded in the distance.

"A fire?" she repeated, sounding dazed. "How? Why?"

Again he asked, "Are you all right?

"I think so. Yes." She licked her lips, drawing his gaze, sending a stab of hunger to his belly.

"Are you sure?"

"I'm a bit dizzy, but otherwise..." She nodded. "I'm fine. Good thing I didn't remove my contacts. If I lost them, I'd be in deep trouble."

He was still holding her at arm's length. "If I let you go, will you behave yourself?"

Tilting her head, she winced, then nodded. "I think so. I'm sorry. Really."

He didn't release her.

Seeing his hesitation, she sighed. "I can't control it. Isn't that awful? I can barely control my own body."

Again, she made no sense. "Now?"

"I've got it under control." But she didn't sound certain.

"Jewel, did you hit your head?"

Frowning, she touched her temples, pushing the hair away from her face. "I don't... no."

"What happened here?" He jerked his head toward the huge fire. "What happened to you?"

"I don't know."

"You don't know how the fire started?"

She shook her head. "No. I was outside and I passed out in the woods. When I came to, I made it back to the house and went inside. All I remember is dropping onto my bed, and then you, awakening me to this."

The roof caved in, sending a shower of sparks high into the sky. The fire roared in triumph.

They were both silent as they stared at the raging inferno that had been her rental house.

"But you don't know how the fire started?" He was nothing if not persistent.

"Someone probably set it." Her tone was flat. "Cutting my brake line didn't work, so they thought they'd kill me in a fire."

Coming from anyone else, he would have said her words were crazy. For Jewel Smith, aka Julie Licciardoni, they made sense.

"You can let me go now," she said.

Feeling guilty, he dropped his arms. "I'm sorry."

"Don't be." She wouldn't look at him as she slowly climbed to her feet. "I'd do the same thing, if someone I found repulsive kept trying to seduce me."

"Repulsive?" Though he knew he should keep his mouth shut, he couldn't help exclaiming at her words. "Believe me, that's the furthest thing from the truth."

The fire engine rounded the corner in a cloud of dust, wheels skidding slightly on the gravel road. Pulling Jewel out of the way, Colton kept his arm around her slender shoulders as they watched the firefighters attempt to beat back the flames with a massive spray of water.

When the fire—and the old Pryor place—had been reduced to smoldering ashes, she looked up at him and shook her head. "I can't believe this."

"They'll find out how it started." He pointed at a tall, stocky man watching as two others put out hot spots. "That's Bill Snow. He's a trained arson investigator."

A moment later the man walked over. He nodded at Colton, then eyed Jewel. "Jewel Smith?"

She nodded. "Did you find out what caused the fire?"

"Yes, I did." Expression grim, he seemed to regard them both with suspicion. "I'll need to ask you a few questions." He looked at Colton. "You, too. This fire was deliberately set."

Jewel froze. She made a sound low in her throat, her shoulders tensing under his hand. "I knew it. Damn it."

Bill took out a pad and pen, eyeing Colton. "You called this in, correct?"

Colton nodded. "I did. I was fishing from my boat when I saw and smelled the smoke."

The other man's gaze swiveled to Jewel.

"What about you? What were you doing when the fire started?"

Trembling from exhaustion, she blinked. She could barely focus on the other man. "I…"

Colton had to set Bill straight. "She was asleep in the house. If I hadn't broken in and dragged her out, she would have died."

Shuddering, Jewel nodded. "I never told you thanks."

He squeezed her shoulder in answer.

Glancing from one to the other, Bill looked confused. "What? If the fire was deliberate, and she was asleep… Are you saying someone tried to kill her?"

"It looks that way." He squeezed her shoulder again. "She definitely thinks so."

Jewel moved restlessly against him. "I know so."

"If that's the case, that would make this arson also an attempted murder. I'll need to notify the police, so they can assign a detective."

Colton nodded. "Good idea."

The other man studied Jewel. "Before you went to sleep, you didn't hear anything or notice anyone suspicious lurking around?"

"No." She looked disgusted with herself. "Not at all. Even once I fell asleep, I should have heard him. I have excellent hearing.

Normally." She swallowed. "This time, I didn't hear a thing."

Colton held his tongue. Of course the fact that she'd been completely unconscious might have had something to do with that.

"I'll inform the police." Putting his pad back in his jacket pocket, Bill looked from one to the other. "They'll probably have a few questions for you both, too. Oh, and Reba will want to talk to you also."

Jewel nodded, swaying on her feet. Colton thought if he took his hand from her shoulder, she'd crumple to the ground.

Bill noticed, too. "What are you going to do now?" His tone softened, though his gaze was still sharply watchful.

"I don't know." Though she didn't look at him, Colton knew what she was thinking. She had no home, no car, nothing. At the very least, she'd need a few days to pull her resources together and figure out what to do.

Colton heard himself answering for her. "She's staying at my place until she decides."

Chapter 6

Standing much too close to Colton but unable to summon the energy to move away, Jewel managed to hold everything together until the fire truck left, taking Bill the arson investigator with it. Then, when Colton gently turned her around and held her, she knew she had to choose between anger— and self-respect—or tears.

Of course she chose the anger, but before she could work up a good rage, the tears came.

She cried for herself and her trapped wolf, for what her life should have been and how it had ended up. She didn't know how much longer she could continue to live like this, unable to change, unable to fight, with no one to turn to.

And then this—Colton's unexpected kindness. Not only was he the most attractive man she'd ever met, but he wanted to be her friend. He'd offered her a place to stay, temporary shelter until she figured out a new path, claiming he wanted nothing in return. She believed him too, especially since she knew men who wanted more would not have hesitated to take advantage when she'd so wantonly offered her body.

He claimed to like her and, while she knew better than to trust him, instinctively she wanted to believe. All that he'd done, especially his actions now, told her he could be trusted.

Unfortunately, until she regained control of her own body, she knew she could not.

Pity party over, Jewel sniffed and wiped at her eyes. Mumbling a quick thanks at Colton, she pushed herself out of his arms, away from him in case her raging libido took over.

Her car was totaled, her rental house gone. What little possessions she'd had had burned. Luckily, she never took her silver wolf necklace off, so she still had that. That, and the clothes on her back.

Ignoring the yellow crime-scene tape and poking through the rubble of what had been her temporary refuge, Jewel jumped when Colton called her name.

"Are you ready to go?" he asked. The gentleness in his tone and the pity she saw in his eyes was nearly her undoing. "I've got my boat."

Straightening, she walked over to him, shading her eyes with her hand. "About that, while I appreciate you making the offer and all, I don't think me staying with you is a good idea."

With the sun behind him, his expression was in shadow, making it difficult for her to read his face. "Don't make any more of it than it is. This would be a temporary thing, just until you get on your feet."

"Thank you, but no."

"Why not?"

Why not? She could give him one big reason. Instead she focused on the one he could relate to. "I keep trying to seduce you, remember? If we're staying together in close quarters, I can't promise it won't happen again."

He looked away at her words. The sudden tension she sensed in him told her he wasn't as immune to her as he pretended to be.

"See," she said gently. "When you think about everything, you can see it's a bad idea."

"You have nowhere else to go."

"True, but that's not your problem."

At her words, he shook his head. "How long has it been since you had a friend?"

To her shame she felt tears sting her eyes. "I haven't had any friends since Leo and I married, and I think you know that."

He took a step toward her, jamming his hands into his pocket. "Let me help you. Let me be your friend."

This she couldn't fathom. "What's in it for you?"

"Having someone as brave and resourceful as you as my friend. You took a stand against what your husband was doing. You were fearless, even when you said you were buying a gun. I admire your courage."

Her throat closed up. She couldn't remember the last time anyone had admired her for anything. In her husband's circles, the only people she'd known for the last five years, she was universally despised.

It had been a long time since she'd had a friend. She so badly wanted to take him up on his offer. But, like everything else about her life here, their tentative friendship was based on lies. True friends didn't have secrets.

Sure, he'd offered to let her stay with him, extended a helping hand in her time of need, but he had no idea what she was—or, more accurately, what she had been. If he found out she was a shifter, once he got past his initial shock, he'd push her away.

Most humans didn't like learning their myths and nightmares were real.

She looked up, met his gaze, and felt as if she were drowning. How he, a human male, could make her melt inside with a simple look, she didn't understand. Most likely this had something to do with the fact that her system was at its weakest, and the wall she'd erected to protect herself was beginning to tumble.

"Jewel?" His voice seemed to come from a long way off. "Are you all right?"

She blinked, realizing she'd been staring, and felt her face color. "I'm fine," she said, feeling as though she were lying again.

"Then you'll stay with me?"

"I—" Maybe she was making too much out of this. A simple offer of friendship could be that, and nothing more.

Partly because she was exhausted, and partly because she knew he was right, she found herself nodding. "Thank you, I will. I appreciate the offer. It means a lot to me."

His smile warmed the cold core inside her. "Great. Are you ready to go?"

She nodded, swaying again on her feet. This exhaustion, brought on by her failed attempt to change, always came after the raging sexual need. "I'll stay with you for a little while, until I figure out what to do."

He took her arm. "You look about ready to fall over."

Stifling a yawn, she lifted her chin. "I am. This…illness takes a lot out of me."

To his credit, he didn't ask. Instead, he helped her onto his boat, untying the anchor before jumping onboard himself.

"We've got to figure out a way to keep you safe," he said, touching her arm. "What I don't understand is, if this is Leo's work, why is he having this sort of thing done? Cutting brake lines and setting fires? I'd think if someone like him wanted to kill you, there'd be much more efficient ways to do it."

Startled, she shot him a glance. Fiddling with the ignition blower switch and other gadgets on his console, he wasn't watching her. Without even knowing her or Leo, Colton had somehow arrived at the truth. A car accident wouldn't have killed her, unless the car had burned. A fire would have; indeed a combination of the two had ended her adoptive parents' lives.

"Torture." She kept her voice emotionless, not

wanting to reveal too much. "Leo thrives on tormenting me. He wants me to know he's found me and plans to make sure I suffer before I die."

Colton's narrow-eyed look contained rage. "What kind of man—" He broke off, visibly collecting himself. "You need protection," he said again.

She thought for a moment, unsure how to respond to the understatement of the year. Deciding a brusque, businesslike approach would be best, she nodded. "I agree. Since I can't leave town without transportation and money, I think I need to learn how to protect myself. I've got to arm myself and learn how to use a gun."

Whatever answer he made was lost over the sound of the boat engine roaring to life. She had to shout to be heard over the noise. "While I'm staying with you, maybe you can teach me how to shoot."

His hands stilled on the wheel. Narrowing his eyes, he studied her. "You're serious about that?"

"I am." She yawned again. "Though not right now. Now, I need to rest."

"All right, then." He used reverse to move the boat back into the water. "Have you already purchased a gun?"

"Not yet." Comfortably seated, she brushed her hair back from her face and looked out over the water shimmering in the moonlight. In another life, she might have found this place beautiful. But not today. Definitely not today. "I'd like you to help me choose the right one, if you don't mind. I'd like a pistol, a revolver, I think."

One hand on the wheel, he guided the boat with a quiet competence. His gaze was cool and clear and gave none of his thoughts away. "Why not an automatic? They're much easier to use."

She gave him the only explanation she could— the truth. "Because silver bullets don't come in cartridges."

Though she could see he wanted to ask, he only shook his head.

He had a boat dock at the edge of his property, and after guiding the boat into the slip, he led her up the path to his house.

At the back door, she stopped, fingering her wolf necklace. "I don't have a change of clothes or a nightgown. Hell, I don't even have toothpaste or deodorant."

After a startled look, he touched her arm. "You're right. Let's make a quick run into town."

Still she balked, not wanting to take even more charity from him, but knowing she had no choice. "I don't have any money."

He brushed a quick kiss on the side of her cheek. Though he'd no doubt meant the kiss to be brotherly, she felt the touch of his mouth all the way to her toes. "This one's on me," he said, leading the way to his truck. "Come on."

By the time they made a stop at Wal-Mart to buy her a couple of changes of clothing and toiletries, including a new contact case and new solution, she felt like a refugee. Since cleaning out her modest checking account before Leo closed it, she'd had to pinch pennies, but she'd never been completely, utterly broke before.

She hated to rely on anyone but herself.

Worse, she was starving. Again. She needed red meat, preferably steak.

Her stomach growled, sounding a little like her caged wolf.

Colton noticed. "I'm hungry too." He smiled. "I'm a mean griller, if I do say so myself. How about a juicy T-bone? I've got a couple of steaks in the fridge."

Like he'd read her mind. She grinned back. "As long as you can cook it rare, I'm game."

"Rare? Not medium rare, but bloody?"

"Exactly." Shifters liked their meat as close to fresh as possible.

Though he raised a brow, he didn't comment further. Instead, he started telling her about the garden he kept in the back of his house. Apparently, it had been started by the home's previous owner, and Colton kept it up for a hobby.

"Last year I gave away more vegetables than I used."

"Rabbit food," she said, smiling. "Sometimes it's good, but I like my red meat."

As they turned into his drive, she caught him giving her a sideways look. Telling herself that what he thought of her didn't matter—after all, he was only human—she clutched her Wal-Mart bag to her chest and kept her gaze resolutely straight ahead.

The sooner she got out of this town, away from these people and this man, the better.

The more time she spent with Colton, the more chance she'd make a mistake and reveal her true nature.

Changing into one of the outfits she'd bought at Wal-Mart, she joined him on the patio.

He grilled the steaks with a quiet competence, serving hers up with a baked potato. Staring at the warm meat, blood oozing around the plate, she had to remind herself to use her fork and knife. She almost picked the T-bone up with her hands and tore into it with her teeth.

The fine line separating her human self from the caged wolf was growing thinner. This then, was what the descent into madness would be like, if she didn't succeed in changing soon.

Such grim thoughts could ruin a perfectly good meal, so she pushed them away, concentrating on the food. Even though she chewed each piece of meat thoroughly, she still finished before Colton, though she'd yet to touch her baked potato.

She had to cover the bone itself with her napkin as her wolf wanted to gnaw. "Very good," she told Colton.

"You *were* hungry," he teased, pausing in the act of cutting another piece from his steak. He had no way of knowing she had to bite her lip to keep from reaching across the table and snatching the rest of his meat from his plate.

Quickly, Jewel focused on trying to eat her baked potato. While she ate that, Colton finished the last of his steak, saving her from possible embarrassment.

Pushing back his chair, he smiled at her. "You've had a tough day. Why don't you go out onto the porch while I clean up?"

He'd built a screened-in porch on the back of his house. Two chaise longues overlooked the lake. Jewel settled into one of them, feeling both content and ill-at-ease.

Instead of relaxing, she should be concentrating on making a new plan of action. Yet, despite her best attempts, Jewel couldn't keep her eyes open. The failed attempt to change, along with the shock of the fire, was too much. Sated from the meal, her body was shutting down.

She was asleep before Colton finished the dishes.

He stood in the doorway and watched her, wondering how she could be such a mysterious bunch of contradictions. To look at her, with her aristocratic features and creamy skin, she belonged in swanky tearooms eating cucumber sandwiches and sipping from fragile china cups. Instead, she ate her steak bloody and wanted to learn how to shoot a gun.

Though she was the sexiest woman he'd ever met, she never dressed provocatively. Instead, she wore clothing that seemed designed to hide her considerable attributes. Yet she'd tried twice to seduce him.

Fascinated by her, seriously in lust with her, he also admired the hell out of her. She was the most resilient person he'd ever met. Since she'd arrived in Anniversary, disaster after disaster had struck her, and she'd simply picked herself up and continued on.

Worse, she'd been right—someone *was* trying to kill her.

Maybe, just maybe, if he used his every resource and called in a few favors, he might be able to find out who.

The next morning, he got ready for work while Jewel slept. He was loath to disturb her this morning, unable to deal with her effect on him, so he let her sleep. Even the sight of her toddling off to bed from the patio had made his mouth go dry.

She didn't awake this morning, despite his puttering around in the kitchen and making coffee. She slept the deep sleep of the truly exhausted. When Reba called to check on her, he'd told the Realtor Jewel was still asleep.

Before heading off to work, he scribbled a note, telling her to help herself to anything in the house and leaving his cell-phone number and a message to call Reba.

Arriving at the newspaper office, Colton barely made it to his desk before the questions started. It seemed everyone knew about Jewel's fire and that the beautiful blonde was staying at his place.

He nearly groaned out loud. How had he managed to forget about small-town gossip?

Hastily, he put together a "no comment" type statement. "It's a temporary thing until she figures out where else to go."

His boss, Floyd, grabbed a chair and sat, straddling it. Of anyone with questions, he was the only person Colton had to answer to. A former hotshot reporter from New Jersey, he'd retired and moved to Texas to run the small newspaper. "Is she in the Witness Protection Program?"

Before Colton could answer, Floyd continued. "Because if she is, then they should be the ones worried about moving her. Not you. You don't want to get involved with something like this, believe me."

"She's not and they're not." He tried to make his answers short and to the point, unwilling to give too much of Jewel's personal life away. As if he knew very much of it, anyway.

Floyd leaned closer. "Let me tell you, Colt. I've lived around these big palookas all my life. People like this Leo Licciardoni, he's got connections everywhere. You follow?"

"I know."

"And you still got involved?" Floyd whistled. "That woman must be something, that's all I've got to say."

"You've never seen her?" Joe Davies and Susan Riddler, two of his co-workers, wandered over. Joe winked at Colton. "She looks like she could be one of those models for that lingerie catalog."

Susan shook her head. "Give her a break. I

heard the fire was deliberate." Her voice signaled she was in full reporter mode. "Do you think the car accident might have been, too?"

"Anything is possible," Colton said in his best gruff, quit-wasting-my-time voice. "Now can I get to work? Believe it or not, I've got stuff to do."

"Think of the story," Susan breathed. "What I wouldn't give to write it."

Eyes bright, Floyd snapped his fingers. "That's it, people. The story of the year has just been dumped in our lap. And we've got a man on the inside to cover it."

They all looked at Colton.

He shook his head. "No can do. Conflict of interest."

Floyd narrowed his eyes. "Bullshit. You've been a major player in a much larger market. Your name on the byline will give this story credibility. I'll bet all the wire services will pick it up. Our little paper can finally grab some recognition. You'll write it."

Because he needed to keep his job, even though he had no intention of exposing Jewel any further, Colton held his tongue. He could stall them, tell Floyd he was working on gaining her trust. That would keep them off track for a little while.

Leaving him free to concentrate on finding out the name of her local enemy.

* * *

No money, no car, no home. Repeating the words like a mantra, Jewel paced the streets of Colton's neighborhood, using exercise as both an outlet for her frustration and a way to stay in shape. Even though she had to keep an eye out for danger, she didn't think anyone would recognize her now. Not only had she chopped off her long hair, but she'd used the last of the money Colton had loaned her to purchase hair dye, and she'd colored it red. Oversize sunglasses and baggy discount-store clothing completed the disguise.

She looked nothing at all like beautiful Jewel Smith, even less like glamorous Julie Licciardoni.

Now, she could come up with a viable plan. First, she needed more money. The only way to get it would be to find a job. Something like waitressing, where she could make instant cash from tips.

One of the numerous restaurants in town might hire her. And, if she could manage to get a morning shift, maybe she could ride to town with Colton.

Energized at the prospect, she began walking toward downtown Anniversary.

A half hour later, perspiring and dehydrated in the blazing sun, she took shelter under a huge pecan tree. If she'd been able to change, she could have made much better time, as well as been able to sniff out water to drink.

As it was, she hadn't even thought to bring bottled water. Ahead, she saw a gas station and convenience store. Since she had no money, she couldn't buy a drink, but maybe they'd have a water fountain inside.

They didn't, but the young clerk took pity on her and gave her a bottle of water on the house. She gratefully drained it before hitting the street again.

The first café she came to wasn't hiring. Neither was the Cajun place or the Catfish buffet. At the third restaurant she tried, Jack's Grill on the Water, which seemed more of a sports bar than anything else, the manager took one look at her and hired her on the spot. "Big Al," as he invited her to call him, accepted her elaborate story of losing all her identification papers in the fire without blinking.

"Can you work tonight?" He handed her a black and white striped referee shirt and a short black skirt. "Do you have a pair of black high heels?"

She nodded. She didn't have a pair of anything except what she was wearing, but he didn't need to know that. She'd get some, somehow. "What time?"

Drumming his fingers on the bar, he tilted his head. "The late shift. Come in around eight. You'll do great. Friday nights, this place is packed. We've got a live band starting at nine."

Biting her lip, Jewel nodded. She still had to tell Colton, but if she could get tips tonight, she could start stashing back some money and planning her escape.

If she could stay alive until then.

Later, after letting herself into Colton's house with the key he'd provided, she poured herself a glass of iced tea and snagged the rocking chair on his front porch. When she spotted his truck heading toward her, she felt a welcoming surge of joy, as though she were suspended in time, the eternal woman, welcoming her mate home.

More foolishness.

As she got to her feet, running one hand nervously through her newly shorn hair and watching Colton climb from his truck and stride toward her, she squashed the urge to run at him, fling herself on him, until they were locked in a deep, drugging kiss.

His first words dispelled that notion entirely.

"What happened to your hair?" Prowling around her as though he were truly a shifter, Colton stared.

Jewel lifted a self-conscious hand to her neck, reminding herself she didn't care what he thought. "I needed a better disguise."

"A disguise?" He shook his head. "You could shave your head and people would still recognize you. Your eyes alone would give you away."

"Then maybe I'll get colored contacts," she snapped. "I'm just trying to stay alive until I can get together enough money to leave, not trying to win a beauty pageant."

His gaze darkened. "Oh, you're still beautiful." The intensity of his eyes pulled her in, keeping her legs rooted to the floor when she wanted to run. "If anything, that short, choppy haircut makes you look even sexier."

"Sexier?" she repeated stupidly, wondering how she could want to kiss a man and slug him all at the same time.

"Uh, yeah." Blinking, he looked away, but not before she saw a hint of red under his tanned skin. "Sorry."

No need to ask what the apology was for—they both felt the strong tug of attraction. She ought to be glad he wanted to resist its pull as badly as she did. Instead, she couldn't help but feel…bereft.

"I got a job," she said, needing to distract them both. "I'm now a waitress at Jack's Grill on the Water."

"Really?" Colton frowned. "I know that place. On the weekends it's the closest thing to a meat market that Anniversary has."

Her wolf stirred with interest, though she knew he didn't mean that literally. "A meat market?"

"Yeah. For guys on the prowl. You'll be bait."

The idea made her smile. Bait? Though Colton didn't know it, as a shifter among humans, she was the predator, never the prey. Her smile faded. Until now. Since she couldn't change, she didn't know what she was anymore.

"I should make good tips then."

"True." He still didn't look happy. She wanted to ask why, but didn't need to open the door to more complications.

Instead, she found herself babbling. "The more tips, the better. I really need the money, you know that. I've got to get another car and buy a gun. I rescued my stash of silver bullets from the glove box of my wrecked car."

"Silver bullets?" He stared. "You mentioned that once before, and I thought you were joking. You're really serious?"

Cursing her slip of the tongue, Jewel nodded.

"And you have a stash?"

"I like being prepared."

"I don't know of any place that sells such a thing, outside of horror novels and the kind of movies designed to make teenage girls hold on to their dates."

She lifted her chin. "You have to search, but there are specialty bullet-makers. Leo buys them there. I stole them from him. If I could have gotten to one of his guns without him knowing, I'd have done that."

"Why silver? Why would he—why would you want something like that? Regular bullets work just fine."

"Not for the kind of beast I'm up against." Again, nothing but truth and again, nothing he'd understand.

"Kind of…" Colton shook his head. "Sometimes you worry me."

"Sometimes I worry myself." She smiled to take the sting out of her words. Her shorn hair felt light and liberating. "I'll work my ass off, save as much as I can, as quickly as I can, and get out of your hair, I promise."

He stiffened. "I never asked you to leave."

"Surely you didn't think I'd mooch indefinitely."

"You're not mooching."

"Whatever." She shrugged. "What else could you call it?"

He looked away, his mouth tight, but not before she'd seen the wounded look in his dark eyes.

"Colton, I appreciate everything you're doing for me."

Now he looked back at her, his expression once

again stone. "I'm not doing anything anyone else wouldn't do."

"Ah, yes you are. You're risking yourself by taking me in, you know."

He crossed his arms. "Oh? How is that?"

"They don't care what they have to do to get me, as long as I'm dead. That's the kind of people they are. If you get in their way, you'll be killed, too."

"I'm not worried." He looked fierce and, like her own people, as if he was hoping they would come after him. As if he welcomed a chance to take them on.

Her inner wolf growled in approval.

Jewel shook her head. Surely her imagination was running away with her. Colton wasn't Pack. Any characteristics he might share with her kind had to be merely wishful thinking.

Wishful thinking? She massaged the back of her neck. What was next? She of all people knew better than to believe in fairy tales. Hellhounds. Had she completely lost her mind?

Colton made her feel things she didn't want, emotions she knew weren't real. Needs and wants and wishes—all projections of a lonely and confused woman.

If only she could change...

Swallowing, Jewel knew she couldn't refuse

her body's need, an urge that was as natural to her as breathing. The time to try again would come sooner than she liked. She could only hope Colton wasn't around when it happened.

Colton. Any way she looked at it, the man was trouble.

She had to get out of his life before they both got hurt.

Inside, her wolf whimpered, feeling the bars of the unwanted cage closing in.

Chapter 7

Colton insisted on driving her to work that night. On the way, they stopped at a discount shoe store so she could purchase a pair of black heels with his money. Money she promised to pay back immediately.

She waited until she was in his truck before she slipped off her flip-flops and put on the new shoes. Colton said nothing, apparently relaxed and calm, though when she glanced over at him, she saw a muscle working in his jaw.

"What's wrong?" she asked, before she thought better of it.

He glanced at her, frowning. "Someone's trying to kill you. I'm afraid you'll be an easy target, working in a public place like Jack's."

"I know." She touched his arm, wondering why she craved contact with him. "But I don't have a choice. You know that."

"I could loan you the money."

Her throat felt tight. "You barely know me."

"That doesn't matter." He lifted one shoulder. "Besides that, I feel like I've known you forever."

"I feel the same way." Again, words slipped out before she could stop them, words she'd had no intention of saying. "Listen, I should clarify something with you before this goes any further. I like you. A lot. But I have no intention of getting involved in any kind of relationship."

"Not ever?" Amusement colored his tone.

"Not now. Maybe not ever."

"Jewel, relax. I just want to be your friend."

She sensed the falseness of his words, an untruth she didn't think he even realized he spoke. He wanted more, she wanted more, and as long as they kept lying to themselves, they might be all right.

Might being the operative word.

"Good," she said, playing along. "Because I just can't handle—"

"I know." Changing lanes, he signaled a right turn. "We're nearly there."

She had fifteen minutes before her shift started. After circling the packed parking lot, Colton finally located a space behind the building.

"Are you ready?" he asked.

Stomach in knots, she nodded. Slipping from his truck, she teetered a bit in the heels before throwing her shoulders back and lifting her chin. Crossing around the back of the truck, Colton joined her, his gaze sweeping over her in a way that sent heat flashing to her belly.

"The shoes look good," he told her, his tone low and decidedly masculine.

"Thanks." If he kept looking at her that way, she knew she would have trouble concentrating on her job. "Maybe you should go."

"Not yet." The smile he flashed her seemed possessive. "I like this place. I think I'll come in and hang out for a while."

Great. They crossed the pavement together. Several customers, all male, turned to stare as she passed.

She felt…exposed. As if she needed to cross her arms over her chest. The low-cut, black-and-white striped referee uniform she'd been given could have come straight from Frederick's of Hollywood. She'd been shocked when she'd got a glimpse of herself in the mirror. Colton had taken one look at her when she'd emerged from the bathroom and his eyes had gone dark, full of heat.

The way they were now.

She shivered. Inside, she felt her wolf self stir and ruthlessly suppressed it. The last thing she needed was another complication, especially one so huge.

Though not yet full dark, the night air felt different from the searing heat of the day. A light breeze blew in off the water, and with her enhanced sense of smell, she could detect more wildlife than the combined scents of fish and smoke and sweat allowed.

She wanted to run free.

Not now. For now, she was a human waitress, in need of tips. Lots of them. Nervously, she smoothed her shirt across her belly and concentrated on her walk. She'd have to learn to strut in the shoes, to play up the uniform for all it was worth.

Even though doing so went against every instinct in her body.

At the entrance, one hand on the door handle, she turned to face Colton, trying again to send him packing. For some reason, this was a spectacle she didn't want him to see. "Thanks for the ride."

He nodded. "No problem. I'll bring you home, too. What time do you get off work?"

She blew her breath out. "I don't know. Could I call you when I need you to pick me up? Or, maybe I could get a ride. I'm thinking I'll be working late, until whatever time this place closes."

"That would be 2:00 a.m." Expression implacable, he stopped her with a touch on her arm. "Are you sure you want to do this?"

Though every instinct screamed no, she nodded. "I have to. You've done more than enough to help me out. I couldn't possibly accept any more."

"All right, then." He pulled open the door. "After you."

Staring up at him with a sinking heart, she realized he meant to stay. The thought crossed her mind that his presence would make her role playing more difficult, though she wasn't sure why. This felt all wrong.

Yet, he wasn't her mate.

She lifted her chin. Her emotions made no sense. Colton wasn't her other half. Neither was Leo. Maybe she was one of those shifters destined to spend her life alone, watching from the sidelines. She had no mate, nor would she. Ever. She was no longer Pack. Right now, she was only Jewel Smith, a mostly human woman made destitute by a fire, needing to work so she could escape and stay alive.

She stepped through the door, keeping her head high.

Instantly, the noise level died from a steady roar to a low hum as everyone turned to stare.

"Hey, baby," one man called out. Someone else whistled.

From her side, Colton glared. "You'd think you'd never seen a new waitress before." His tone contained a warning.

"Not one that good-looking." The man who'd whistled stood. Two of his buddies instantly dragged him back down.

Her new boss, Big Al, materialized from the back. "I don't want any fights in here," he warned Colton.

"And I need this job," she seconded. Taking a deep breath, she headed toward the kitchen.

After a brief conversation with Colton, Big Al followed.

"Everyone, gather around," he hollered. "Cooks, waitresses, barkeeps, all of you." Then, one by one, he introduced her to her new co-workers.

After the fifth name, Jewel knew she'd never remember. She focused on the names of the three other waitresses. Sarah, a dark haired woman, was about Jewel's age, while Jolene and Carrie Ann were much older. The two bartenders on duty that night seemed pleasant enough, as did the cooks and dishwashers and busboys. Once Al showed her how to punch the time clock and explained what was expected of her, she was handed a pad and pencil and put to work.

The rest of the night passed in a blur. But always, though he wasn't in her section, she was conscious of Colton sitting at a table in the back, nursing a beer and watching her.

Somehow, he made her feel protected. Foolish, she knew, and even more unwise to enjoy the feeling.

While running trays of drinks out to the crowded, mostly male tables wasn't difficult, it was exhausting. A few hours into the evening, Jewel's back ached and her thighs and calves felt swollen.

Carrying a tray loaded with beers to a rowdy group of city workers, Jewel spotted a familiar face. The man who reminded her of Leo's friends, the man Colton had met for lunch. Sitting alone at a table. Watching her.

Prickles of alarm skittered down her spine.

Jolene brought him a beer and Jewel managed to turn away. What was he doing here? Did Colton know?

The next time she was able to glance his way,

she got her answer. Colton had joined him. Heads bent, the two men talked earnestly.

A customer called her name and she spent the next several minutes filling orders and carrying drinks. When she looked up again, Colton sat alone.

By the time last call was announced, her feet were swollen, too. Her entire body ached.

"So what'd you think?" Sarah asked, handing her a container of salt so she could began refilling the shakers.

"I didn't realize I was so out of shape." Jewel smiled ruefully.

"There's a lot of running around," Carrie Ann agreed. "But with the way they were tipping, I think it'll have been worth the pain."

"Amen to that." Jolene patted her pockets. "Maybe I can make my house payment after all."

The others laughed.

"Your man is still waiting out there for you." Big Al finished drying the last of the beer mugs and slung his towel over his shoulder.

Her man? Jewel felt her face heat.

"Poor Colton." Jolene nudged Carrie Ann. "He probably only had three beers all night."

"Is he driving you home?" Sarah asked.

"Yes."

"Ketchups all refilled," Big Al announced. "Salt and pepper shakers?"

"Done." Carrie Ann grinned. "I'm thinking we might get out of here fairly early tonight."

"Early?" Jewel glanced at the clock. She had to stifle a yawn. More than an hour had passed since closing time. "Three-thirty in the morning?"

"Seems mighty early to me." Still grinning, Big Al pushed through the swinging doors. "Come on, y'all. Let's get out of here so I can lock up."

The scent of smoke still overpowering her nostrils, Jewel followed him, her gaze immediately going to the back table, looking for Colton.

The table was empty.

Stunned, she turned a slow circle. No one but the employees occupied the bar.

"Looking for me?"

She felt a rush of warmth at the sound of his voice behind her. She couldn't believe she hadn't heard his approach, or detected his scent. But then her ears were still throbbing from the sound of the band's amplifiers and all she could smell was smoke.

Instead of answering, she flashed him a grateful smile.

"Are you ready?" At her nod, he took her arm and led her to the truck. She held herself stiffly, a hundred questions swirling in her mind. Only when he'd started the engine and pulled out into the road did she open her mouth.

"Who was that man?" she asked, trying for nonchalance and aware she failed mightily. "The guy you were sitting with at table fifty-three?"

"Fifty-three, huh?" Colton smiled. "That was an old buddy of mine. We used to work together down in Houston. He's trying to get me to go back to my old job."

She let her shoulders sag with relief. "He looks like he could be one of Leo's associates."

"Roy? Don't worry about him—he's harmless." Giving her shoulder a brief squeeze, Colton turned up the radio. The strains of a soft country ballad filled the cab.

On the drive home, she must have dozed. The next thing she knew, Colton was shaking her shoulder, his breath warm on her cheek.

"Wake up."

Blinking, she sat up and dragged her fingers through her hair. "Are we there already?"

"Yep." Climbing out, he crossed to her side and opened her door. As she slid down, he steadied her, and she fought the unreasonable urge to slide into his arms, belly to belly, chest to chest.

His swift intake of breath told her he somehow knew.

"Good night," she told him, shaking off his touch and staggering toward the house. When she reached her room, she peeled off her smoke-scented clothing and fell into bed, grateful for the feel of the clean sheets.

If she dreamed at all, she didn't remember. When sunlight streaming through the window woke her, she glanced at the bedside clock and smiled.

She'd slept in. It was nearly noon. She should have the house to herself since Colton would have gone to work long ago.

Sitting up in bed, she flexed her arms, then her legs, wondering at their soreness. She wasn't used to spending so much time on her feet.

Her pockets, however, were full, stuffed with tips. Though she knew Colton felt uncomfortable with her job, for the first time in months she felt confident, as if she just might have a chance at beating Leo after all.

The day looked promising. She worked again that night, which meant more tips.

Reba called and they chattered awhile until the Realtor's other line beeped and she had to take that call. Jewel was pleased, feeling as though she might have made the first girlfriend she'd had in years.

But as she padded to the bathroom to hop into a nice hot shower, her wolf made itself known. The beast was not pleased.

Staggering, Jewel clutched the edge of the footboard. The wolf fought for freedom, using teeth and claws. With a cry, Jewel fell to the floor, her body jerking with violent spasms. This felt wrong—*was* wrong. She couldn't change now, her body still wasn't ready. Whatever Leo had done to her still hadn't left her system.

Her wolf cared nothing about that. Too long denied, the beast wanted to run, to hunt, to break free.

"No!" she cried out again, loudly. Too loudly.

"Jewel?" Colton's voice.

Damn. What was he doing home? Belatedly, she remembered it was Saturday.

"Jewel?" Closer now. Any moment she expected to see her doorknob turn and her door open.

She couldn't let him see her.

"Yeah." Somehow she managed to respond. "I'm okay. Just…that time of the month." A boldfaced lie, but one virtually guaranteed to stop any man dead in his tracks.

Evidently it worked.

"I'll be in the kitchen," he said. "I'll make another pot of coffee."

"Sounds good," she managed to say, teeth

clenched. Her entire body shuddered as another tremor shook her.

"Not here, not now." She had to struggle to breathe, to keep her bones from lengthening. One finger popped as her nails turned into claws. Her left hand—too late; already a paw. This could be good—she hadn't gotten that far before—if the rest of her body would only follow.

Instead, pain knifed through her, ripping her apart.

"Nooooo…" This time she remembered to keep her voice down.

Her wolf-self fought for all it was worth, desperate for release, for freedom. Equally determined to keep it caged, Jewel fought back, aware the inner struggle was ripping her apart.

How much longer she could go without trying to change, she didn't know.

Finally, the wolf acquiesced.

Gasping, tears running down her cheeks, Jewel climbed to her feet and staggered into the shower. Water on hot, she turned the spray full force, wishing she could wash away whatever curse or poison Leo had used to infect her.

Drying off, she touched her silver wolf necklace for luck and got dressed. Choosing to let her hair air-dry, she studied herself in the bathroom mirror, decided she'd pass for human, and headed to the kitchen where coffee and Colton awaited.

She'd never seen a man look so good in jean cutoffs. Back to her, he fiddled with something on the kitchen counter. Pausing in the doorway, she let her gaze drink in the sight of him. The shorts rode low on his hips, showing a hint of his red cotton boxers. His muscular legs were tanned and he wore black flip-flops. His T-shirt fit well, showing off his toned arms and…

He turned, catching her studying him, and smiled. She felt the force of that smile like a punch to her solar plexus. Damn.

"Good morning."

Somehow she managed to respond. "Morning. Have you been up long?"

His smile widened. "Since about eight. I ran into town and brought you something." He indicated a metal box, the same one he'd been fiddling with when she'd arrived.

Her heart stuttered. "A gift? You shouldn't have."

"I wanted to." He waved his hand. "Go ahead, open it."

She didn't move. Though he had no way of knowing, in her previous life with Leo, a gift always meant a service she had to perform as repayment, usually something painful and humiliating. With Leo, nothing was ever free.

But this was Colton. Searching his craggy face, she saw no hidden malice in his easy smile.

"Go ahead, look at it," he urged. "I think you'll be pleased."

She wanted to, oh how she wanted to. But years of training usurped her desire and instead, unable to help herself, she backed away, shaking her head. "No thanks, I'll pass."

His smile faltered, then disappeared. "Jewel?" Narrow-eyed, he stared. "What's wrong?"

Gritting her teeth, she forced herself to stand still and to look at him, though she couldn't quite manage to stop the fine tremors than ran through her. Inside, her ever-vigilant wolf raised her head. "No gifts, okay?"

"What?" Tilting his head, he studied her face. When comprehension dawned, his frown cleared. He took a step toward her, then stopped. "This has to do with Leo, doesn't it?"

All she could do was nod.

"My God, what did he do to you?"

She took a deep, shuddering breath, then another, clearing her throat before she could speak. "How did you know?"

"It was written all over your face, in your eyes.

You look haunted. Afraid. Despite everything that's happened to you, I've never seen you look like that. What the hell did that bastard do?"

To her credit, she managed to force a smile. "Believe me, you don't want to know."

"Believe me, I do."

"I don't want to talk about it." Despite her unreasonable terror, she couldn't look away from the box on the counter. "Please, take that thing, whatever it is, and put it away."

"It's a gun, Jewel." His voice was quiet. "And, if it will make you feel better, it's not a gift, it's a loan, all right? I went to the gun shop at lunch the other day and filled out the paperwork. The waiting period was up today, so I bought it."

Her throat closed up and she couldn't speak.

"If you're going to work in public, you need to protect yourself."

She nodded, torn between wanting to run away and the opposing desire to turn into his arms and let him hold her.

Her wolf snarled.

"A gun," she said. "An honest-to-goodness gun."

"Yeah. Let me get it for you." Moving slowly, carefully, he crossed the room to the metal box and clicked the latch. Inside, nestled in a bed of foam, was a shining silver pistol, with a wood handle.

The weapon looked both beautiful and deadly.

Drawn, despite herself, Jewel forced her feet to move. A loan, not a gift. Still, the wolf inside shifted restlessly. "What kind..." Clearing her throat, she tried again. "What kind is it?"

"Smith & Wesson revolver, .45 caliber."

She couldn't look away from the weapon. "I thought you preferred an automatic."

He shook his head. "You said you didn't want one. After thinking about it, I realized you were right. Personally, I've always preferred a good revolver. When you handle a gun like this, you know you've got something solid and deadly. Take it out, see how it feels in your hand," Colton said. "It's not loaded."

"Good." But she didn't move.

"Go ahead, touch it."

Tentatively, she stroked the cold metal. "Will you teach me to use it?"

"Of course."

"Then what? I take some test, so I can be licensed to carry?"

"You have to complete the course." He smiled. "Luckily for you, I'm certified to teach it."

Her shock must have shown in her expression. He hadn't mentioned this the last time they'd discussed her getting a license.

"I took the instructor course," he told her. "It helped that I was a crack shot."

"Once I get licensed, I can carry it with me all the time, right?"

"Yes. You'll need to keep your concealed weapon permit with you, too."

Only in Texas. For the first time, her smile felt real, instead of as if her face were cracking. "I'll need to carry my own bullets. I won't use them to practice, but I need to keep them with me."

"Your own—?" Whatever he'd been about to say, he cut off. "Not the silver-bullet thing again."

At her nod, he sighed. "I've never seen them, not at any gun store here or in Dallas. And finding them in the right caliber? You have to make sure they'll fit."

"I know." She smiled glumly. "Luckily, I kept a box or two of .45 caliber bullets. That's what I retrieved from my glove box. They appear to have survived the wreck. Those will work, right?"

"Right. But what happens when you run out?"

"I won't. I only need to use them in special situations." She prayed he wouldn't ask.

Evidently, he'd learned his lesson. "But when you need more, what will you do? They won't be easy to find."

"They never are. The Internet can be helpful. I

can have them custom made." She shrugged, avoiding meeting his gaze.

"And people make them for you, without question?"

She nodded. "The ones that do know what they're for."

Crossing his arms, he studied her. Now he did ask. "And that would be?"

"They're for special hunting." Something must have flashed in her eyes, a darkness that turned his expression hard. Still, she couldn't help that. Even if she could explain, he'd never understand.

"You know, a horrible thought just occurred to me. These silver bullets you have, you didn't get those from your husband's arsenal did you? They weren't cop killers, were they?"

"Cop killers?" She frowned, not familiar with the term. "Yes and no, though I'm not sure what you mean. I got these from his stash, but I'm not familiar with the term *cop killer.*"

"Body armor–piercing bullets."

When she shook her head again, he sighed. "What are you not telling me?"

Even to herself, her laugh sounded forced. Hollow. "Please. No more questions."

"For now, I'll let it go." He took a step closer,

but didn't touch her. "You should know I'll keep searching and digging, until I have answers."

She stared. "Why?"

Now his smile matched her earlier laugh. Completely and utterly false. That smile hurt worse than any blow.

"Why? Because." He shrugged. "Reporters are like that. I'm a reporter. Nothing personal. I just can't help myself."

Chapter 8

An hour later, Colton drove Jewel to self-defense class. Since she'd paid a month in advance, she didn't have to worry about the bill. At least for now.

Everyone stopped what they were doing and stared when she and Colton walked in.

"Small town," he muttered. "Keep your head up and don't let it bother you."

"Okay." She swallowed. "You could leave now, you know."

"No. I'm going to spar a bit, too," he said, doing a much better job than she of pretending not to notice the attention they were getting.

At the end of the lobby, he glanced down at her. "See you later."

Something in his expression made her catch her breath. She couldn't reply, couldn't speak. All she could do was nod and stare helplessly after him as he headed back toward the men's dressing room.

From the other side of the room, a woman screeched. "Yoo-hoo! Jewel!"

Suddenly realizing she was standing in the gym entrance, Jewel raised her head. Reba. Making a beeline for her, the other woman looked intent.

"Come here, girl," she cried, grabbing Jewel's arm and practically dragging her toward the women's room. "Spill all."

"All what?"

"What on earth is going on with you?" The other woman's eyes sparkled with interest.

Jewel pretended ignorance. Shaking her head, she sighed. "I'm surviving."

"I'll say. Since our phone conversation was so short, and then I had to take that other phone call, we didn't get to finish talking. Tell me everything."

"Everything? You already know everything. Have you heard any word from the owners of my rental cabin?"

"Not yet. They have more money than they know how to use." Reba dismissed the entire incident with an unconcerned wave of her many-ringed hand. "And since you appear to have survived the car crash, I'm more interested in what's happening with you and Colton. When I talked to you last, you were just staying there short term. Now I hear around town that you've moved in."

Jewel sighed. Small towns never changed. East or west, north or south, they were all the same. She should have known she couldn't get away with any secret for very long.

"Nothing's going on." Though she spoke truth, her denial sounded weak, even to her own ears.

"You're living with him." Reba stabbed a scarlet nail at Jewel's shoulder.

Instinctively, she flinched. Marriage to a man like Leo did that to a woman. "I'm only staying with him until I figure out what to do."

"Oh, no you don't." Gripping her arm, Reba led her over to the two chairs in the ladies' room sitting area. "I know better than that. I've seen the way you look at him."

Preferring to stand, Jewel searched the other woman's heavily made-up face. "What do you mean?"

"Whenever he's around, you go all dreamy-eyed. And he watches you like a hawk. Remember that story I told you?"

"About his wife and daughter? He mentioned that."

Reba's eyes went big. "He did, did he? Everyone says Colton Reynolds never talks about his past."

Jewel shrugged, letting that one go. "He did to me. Anyway, he was kind enough to offer me a place to stay until I figure out what to do. I lost everything in the fire. He's just helping me out."

With an inelegant snort, Reba disputed that. "Right. But listen, there's something more about Colton you need to know."

"Stop." Jewel held up her hand. "No gossip."

"This isn't gossip. It's fact." Reba leaned closer, narrowing her eyes. "The man's dangerous."

"Reba." For the first time, Jewel let a hint of her savage other self show in her gaze. "Enough."

Reba gasped and took a step backward. Then, recovering her equilibrium, she snagged hold of Jewel's arm. "Are you sure you—?"

"I'm sure." Jewel continued to stare until the Realtor dropped her hand.

"Fine. If you want me to drop it, I will. For now."

"Good." Jewel turned to go. The class would be starting soon.

Reba cleared her throat. "Let me say this much. As long as you aren't involved with Colton, I don't think you're in danger."

Danger. As if. The woman had no idea where Jewel had been. "I'm not involved with him."

"Whatever you say. But I don't believe you, you know."

Jewel sighed. "It's the truth." She turned to go.

"Come on, Reba. The class will be starting soon."

"I know, but I need to tell you about the fire. Since I rented the house to you, I needed to know what to tell the owners when I did reach them. I've talked to the fire department. Have they called you?"

"No."

"The fire was definitely arson. Whoever started it used an accelerant, gasoline."

"I was inside, sleeping." Jewel shook her head. "If Colton hadn't seen the smoke and gotten me out, I would have died."

Reba gasped. "Seriously? No one told me that."

Jewel nodded, waiting for the woman to make the connection. A second later, she did.

"But if it was arson, and they knew you were asleep inside... Are you saying someone tried to kill you?"

"That's what it looks like at this point."

Reba grabbed her arm, her scarlet nails standing out like fresh blood. "But why, honey? Why would anyone want to do that?"

Surprised, Jewel eyed the other woman. Maybe the small-town gossip wasn't as efficient as she'd thought. "Because of who I am, what I did."

"What did you do? Who'd you piss off?"

"I'm…" She couldn't go on. Jewel tried another tack. "You don't recognize me from television? Several other people around town did."

"Really? You were on TV?" With a bewildered expression, Reba studied her. "I'm sorry, but I don't recall seeing you. Who are you and what did you do?"

While Jewel tried to decide how best to answer, the bathroom door swung open and two other women strolled in, chatting. They caught sight of Reba clutching Jewel and hurried over.

"We've heard the most delicious gossip." Brown eyes sparkling, the older woman with the tight gray curls grinned. "We had no idea we had a celebrity in our midst."

"I'm not a—"

"You know who she is?" Looking from one to the other, Reba sounded dismayed. "I guess I should, but I really don't have any idea."

The second woman tittered. "Tsk, tsk."

"I was about to tell her," Jewel protested weakly, the woman's heavy perfume making her nose twitch and her eyes water. She tried to smile, all the while wishing she could break and run for it. Sometimes being a wolf was much simpler.

Except when the wolf wanted to break free of the unwanted cage.

Blinking, she realized both Reba and the other woman were staring. She patted Reba's shoulder. "I'll let her tell you all about it. Maybe we can get together after class." With that, she hurried off to join the other students, leaving Reba and her friend to trail after her.

After the class, she avoided Reba, not wanting to rehash her sad story, and went to meet Colton, stretching her pleasantly aching muscles.

"Are you ready?" Colton smiled. Jewel smiled back, wondering how his every smile could affect her so.

Instead of heading home, he drove them to a local shooting range.

"I thought you might practice," he said, pulling into a parking spot near the front door. "I brought the gun." Opening the glove box, he removed the metal case and held it out to her.

Jewel stared, an unreasonable trepidation filling her. Hesitantly, she took the case, swallowing hard. "Okay."

"Don't look so scared. The sooner you can protect yourself, the better. At least for now you can get a feel for the pistol, the weight of it, the way it fires."

He was right, of course, but she hated feeling so unprepared. She wasn't ready, yet in another way, she'd never been more ready.

Though Leo had hired someone to torture her, she knew it wouldn't be long before he decided to kill her. "You're right." Holding the case gingerly, she got out of the car.

"You don't have to carry that as though it's going to break," he pointed out, smiling.

"Oh? I guess I'm more afraid I might accidentally set it off."

"No bullets." His grin widened. "It's not loaded."

Signing them both in to the firing range, he snagged ear protectors. Once they were in their stall, he showed her how to load the gun, how to remove the safety and how to sight the target.

"Now squeeze the trigger and be ready. There's a bit of a backlash when it fires."

As Jewel did as he directed, she felt an icy calm steal over her, similar to the way she felt when, as a wolf, she'd had prey within striking range.

"Steady," Colton murmured. "Now shoot."

Aiming for the paper outline's heart, she complied. Despite his warning, the recoil surprised her, though it wasn't painful.

"Direct hit." He patted her shoulder. "Now go again."

So she did. She shot again and again, learning how to reload the chamber, developing a comfortable familiarity with the revolver. One box of bullets, gone. She took a break, lowered the gun, before asking for another.

Without question, he handed her the second box of ammunition. "You're pretty good at this."

Sighting the revolver, Jewel smiled grimly. "I'd better be." She squeezed the trigger, hitting the paper target at just above its heart.

"Natural talent." Colton sounded pleased. "But you'll need to finish up. We've got to go."

"Go?" She glanced at her watch, surprised to see it was nearly seven. "You're right. I wasn't aware so much time had gone by. We've got to head back. I need to get dressed for work."

"Another full shift?"

Was that censure in his voice? Jaw tight, she nodded. "I'm working as many hours as they'll let me." Checking the safety, she handed the gun to him, butt first. "Thanks. That was intense. I enjoyed myself."

His expression shuttered, he placed the pistol in the case. "I could tell." His tone was bleak, making her realize she'd confused him further.

During their ride home, rather than trying to explain, she stared out the window until they reached his house.

As she got out of the truck, he called her name.

She waited while he crossed to her.

His dark gaze searched her face. "Tell me the truth. Have you used a weapon before?"

So that was it. The tightness around her chest lightened. "Honestly, no."

He didn't move. "I know about your husband's reputation. There are rumors about how many people he's murdered."

"*Ex*-husband." A spark of anger flared. "His actions had nothing to do with me. Up until the end, I didn't even know what he did. You don't understand—I was Leo's prisoner, not his partner."

He kissed her then, slanting his mouth across hers in a ruthless, hard way that would have cowed a lesser woman. But she was a shifter and strong, and she met his urgency, deepening the kiss. As her arousal grew, she realized she welcomed him the way she would have welcomed a long absent mate.

Mate?

The thought was like a dash of cold water in the face.

Ripping herself away, she ignored the flash of

hurt in his face. "I've got to get ready to go to work." She ran for his house. He followed at a distance.

Stepping aside to allow him to unlock the door, she tried to slow her breathing and calm her racing pulse.

Fumbling with the door and his key, Colton didn't look at her. His breathing sounded loud and harsh, as erratic as hers, telling her she had the same effect on him. As soon as he turned the lock, she dashed inside.

Alone in her room, she closed the door and, panting, sat down on the edge of the bed. Her hands shook, little tremors that both infuriated and frightened her. How was this possible, that Colton Reynolds affected her so violently?

She didn't need this sort of complication in her life. Staying alive would take every resource she had.

Pulling on the microscopic, stretch miniskirt, along with her black heels, Jewel smoothed down her referee shirt, dropped her silver wolf necklace inside the neck, and peered at herself in the mirror. She looked like someone entirely different from the woman she'd once been. More confident, less soft. Leo had made her timid, ripping her natural confidence from her like a leaf from a tree.

She liked to think she'd regained herself. She would believe it, too, if only she could change.

Inside, her wolf snarled in agreement. This inability to allow her other self force must be why, despite her marksmanship lessons with Colton, she didn't look at all like the fierce and excellent huntress she'd once been.

She wanted to be that huntress again.

Worriedly, she realized her wolf had been especially restless lately. Perhaps simply licking her wounds, but she knew that when the wolf made another attempt at freedom, the urge would be a powerful one. The more time that passed, the more the urge would gain strength. Soon, she would have no choice but to try again.

When she emerged from her bedroom, Colton waited, lounging against the kitchen counter. The heat darkening his gaze reminded her of his kiss, and she felt her entire body respond.

"Ready?" He fished his truck keys from his pocket.

"Sure." Face burning, she brushed past him on the way out the door.

They made the short drive into town in silence.

As he pulled into a parking space, she turned to look at him. "You don't have to stay."

"I know." He gave her a grim smile. "But I want to."

Though she knew she shouldn't ask, her tongue seemed to run away with her mouth. "Why?"

"Someone's got to protect you."

"I can protect myself." Normally, this would be an absolute truth. Even though she couldn't yet shift, she retained her above-average strength.

He shook his head. "Not yet, you can't. Are you ready? I'll walk you inside."

Feeling oddly self-conscious, she nodded. "I'm not sure I like this," she told him, as they headed for the entrance to the bar. "I'm not used to having someone try and protect me."

Colton stopped dead in his tracks. "That bastard," he swore. "He was your husband. If any man should ever take care of a woman, a husband should."

She reached for the door handle before he could, yanking it open and heading into the noise without replying.

Again, the bar was packed, even by the time she arrived for her nine-to-close shift. A popular, local band warmed up in preparation for their set. Lifting her hand in a quick wave, Jewel headed for the kitchen. She'd barely punched in when Big Al approached her.

"Your section is gonna be twice as large as the one you worked last night," he warned.

"The tips should be good." Jewel nodded at Jolene as she edged past, balancing a heavy tray full of schooners of beer.

"Yep. As long as you work 'em." Al wiggled his eyebrows.

"I plan to." Jewel grinned back. She liked the big man.

"Then you'd better get a move on." He clapped three times. "Chop, chop," he said, winking at her before hurrying away.

Smile fading, Jewel tied on her change pouch, grabbed a pad and pencil and headed out into the crowded room.

Instinctively, she looked for Colton. There he was, in Jolene's section, at his usual corner table near the back of the room.

"Honey, bring me some liquor!" one of her customers hollered. She hurried over to a boisterous table full of older men, scribbling down their orders as fast as she could.

With a crash of drums and echoing guitar, the band launched into their first song, a spirited rendition of an old Buddy Holly tune. The noise level grew past a roar and Jewel's head began to ache.

Scurrying to keep her customers supplied with

alcohol and food, she lost sight of Colton in the crush of orders and drinks and dodging an occasional attempt to pinch or squeeze.

Concluding their first song to cheers, the band began a second. They were loud, raucous and played classic rock on request. The tiny dance floor quickly filled.

Jewel sneezed from the smoke. And her nose wasn't the only thing affected—her sensitive hearing would be sorely abused before the night was over. Even now, each beat of the drum reverberated inside her head.

Head down, she barreled for the kitchen—and right into a woman customer.

"I'm so sorry." She had to shout to be heard. Raising her head, she realized the woman was Reba, dressed in a black leather miniskirt and teal silk halter top. She'd completed her daring outfit with huge teardrop earrings and enough eyeliner to make her look five years older.

"Hey!" Reba shouted. "This is a happening place."

Readjusting her tray, Jewel jerked her head in a nod. "It is. What are you doing here? I didn't know you liked this kind of thing."

Reba didn't smile. "We've got to talk." Grabbing Jewel's arm, she pulled her toward the ladies' room.

"I'm working," Jewel protested. "Can't it wait until later?"

"Not hardly, hon." Grim-faced, she steered Jewel down the hall.

Once they pushed through the door into the restroom, it felt as though they'd entered a sanctuary.

"Much better." A hard look from Jewel had Reba dropping her hand. "I'm sorry to bother you here, but this couldn't wait."

"What's wrong?"

"Colton, that's what's wrong."

"Not this again." This time, Jewel didn't bother hiding her annoyance. "He's helping me out. Doing me a favor. He's asked for nothing in return. Get it?"

"You heard about his wife, right? You said he told you."

"I know his daughter died of an overdose and his wife went to jail." Glancing at her watch, Jewel shook her head. "Why? What does any of this have to do with me?"

"Because, now that I know who you are, I know you have to be careful."

The words stopped Jewel cold. Had she finally located her enemy?

Not good. They were alone and Jewel wasn't armed.

"What do you mean?" she asked carefully.

Reba reached to touch her, but drew back her arm at the last moment. "Honey, I read up on your story. Your husband, that Leo, he was a gangster and he abused you, didn't he?"

"Ex-husband." Jewel crossed her arms, refusing to lower her gaze. There was no point in denying what had become, to her shame, public knowledge. "Yes, he did. Why?"

Reba took a deep breath and swallowed. "Because Colton Reynolds could be the same type of man. I've recently heard that he abused his wife, too. And had an affair. That's what drove her to try drugs."

Unable to help herself, Jewel laughed. "That's ridiculous."

"I know it sounds unbelievable. But…did you know your ex was abusive when you married him?"

"Of course not."

Pausing for a moment to let her point sink in, Reba swooped in for the kill. "I know you're only staying with him because he offered and you have no place else to go, but I've got an extra bedroom. You're welcome to stay with me."

"I thought you were Colton's friend."

"I was—I am." Reba swallowed. "But I'd like to think that I'm your friend, too. Right now, I'm going on hearsay and trying to give him the benefit of the doubt, but if he ever hurt you…"

Jewel stared at the other woman, resisting the urge to rub her temples. The awful pounding in her head made thinking difficult. Nothing Reba said seemed real. Outside the ladies' room, there were customers waiting and tips to be made. That was her reality right now.

"Jewel?" Reba asked. "Are you all right?"

"I'm fine. Look, I appreciate your concern and all, but Colton's been nothing but kind to me. Since I have no plans to enter into a relationship with him, I don't think I have anything to worry about."

"Think about it, okay?"

"I will," Jewel said, snatching her tray off the counter. No way could she think about this right now. "Seriously, I've got to get back to work."

The five minutes she'd spent in the bathroom meant two of her tables had nearly run out of beer, three food orders had come up, and Big Al was waiting in the kitchen, scowling.

"What happened to you?"

She rolled her eyes. "Woman's crisis in the ladies' room."

Loading three burger specials onto her tray, he snorted. "Are you okay?"

"I'm fine." She lifted the tray and headed back

to the crowded main room. "I'll come back for the others in a sec."

Over the next several hours, Jewel gained a new appreciation for the waitstaff of the world. She'd never worked so hard in her life. Her feet ached, her back hurt and the ever-present headache threatened to burst her skull. Her one consolation, besides the free-flowing tips, was the fact that her wolf stayed docile inside her.

With an hour to go before last call, and several of her tables empty, Jewel finally got to take a breather. The band had gone on break and the noise level was a hum rather than a roar.

Scouting the room, she spotted Colton at the back table, alone. The two guys he'd eaten burgers with earlier had long since gone. She grabbed one of the empty chairs and sat, wincing as her back twinged.

"Long night?"

She nodded. "Yes. And it's not over yet." Jingling her pockets, she gave him a tired smile. "Though I think I did really well in tips."

"Jewel, come here." Big Al appeared in the kitchen doorway. "There's been a mix-up on an order."

Pushing herself off the chair, she sighed. "Back to work I go. I'll see you later."

"I'll be here."

She got the food order straightened out, brought coffee to a few of her tables, and chatted briefly with the band's lead singer as he was about to climb back onstage.

When he asked for her phone number, she shook her head. "I'm sorry, I'm with him." And she pointed at Colton.

As she did, there was a huge crash, a booming sound that reverberated and shook the entire building. The next instant, a car came smashing through the side wall. Tables were upended as people leaped out of the way. Brick and wood collapsed and the wall came down in a shower of debris.

Exactly where Colton had been sitting.

Chapter 9

Using every ounce of her substantial strength, Jewel pawed through bricks and lumber, tossing them to the side.

"Help me," she called to one man, but he wandered off in shock, stumbling toward fresh air and safety.

"Ma'am, you've got to come outside."

Not comprehending, she looked up. A man in a yellow firefighter uniform reached for her arm to help her up.

She bared her teeth in a wolf's snarl.

"I need some help with this one," the fireman called, not taking his gaze from her.

"You don't understand. I think someone's buried under here." Resuming her digging, she glanced back up. "Please, please help me. We've got to get him out."

Dragging a soot-blackened hand across his mouth, he shook his head. "If anyone's under there, it's doubtful he's alive."

With all the fierceness of a she-wolf protecting her mate, she glared him down. "You don't know that. You can't know for certain until we find him. Last time I heard, you have a duty to save lives. Either help me, or get out of my way."

After another second of hesitation, he began pulling at the rubble with her. Soon, two more firefighters joined them.

"There he is," she cried. "I've found his leg."

Not caring who saw, she continued using every bit of her extra strength, tossing bricks and boards and pieces of shingles. A moment later, they had his torso freed, then his arms, and lastly, his head.

"Is he…"

Gently, the first firefighter pushed her aside. "This is my job, ma'am. I'm a trained paramedic. Let me check him."

Keeping a grip on Colton's hand, she moved aside. "He's breathing."

"Pulse is steady. I don't see any blood, or any visible external injuries."

"Maybe he was knocked unconscious by debris." They ignored her.

"We need a stretcher and an IV. This one's going to Athens."

The other two men sprinted off.

"Athens?" Jewel continued to massage Colton's tanned fingers. "To the hospital there?"

"Exactly." The firefighter met her gaze. "Now, if you want to help your friend, you need to stay out of our way, understand?"

She nodded, releasing Colton's hand.

"His vitals look good." He winked at her. "I'm hoping it's only a concussion, nothing really serious. But we won't know until we have him thoroughly checked out, okay?"

She bit her lip. "I understand."

The other two men returned with a stretcher. Gently, carefully, they loaded Colton on it and carried him away. Jewel followed.

"Wait." A medic blocked her way. "Are you family?"

"No, I'm…" She bit her lip. "I'm a good friend."

"Then you can't ride in the ambulance. If you

want to check on him, you can meet us at East Texas Medical Center, 2000 South Palestine." Closing the double doors, he went around to the driver's side, started the engine and sped off, lights flashing.

Dazed, Jewel turned left, then right, looking for someone, anyone she knew.

She found Big Al and the other employees outside, huddled around each other in the parking lot.

"All accounted for, now." The big man enveloped her in a hug. "How's Colton?"

She shivered. "I don't know. They said his vitals were good, but they took him to Athens. I...have no way of getting there."

"I'll take you." Jolene stepped forward, her lined face showing the strain. "As soon as we make sure all the customers got out, okay?"

Grateful, Jewel nodded. Glancing around the parking lot, she saw other clusters of people, standing in tense groups, talking and watching the drama unfold.

She wanted to help, but knew in the confusion and the crush of police officers and firefighters, the best thing they could all do was stay out of the way.

Colton. She had to get to Colton, to stay with him. A mate's place was by his side.

Immediately, she shut down the random thought.

Colton wasn't her mate. They weren't even lovers. They were good friends, nothing more.

"Are you all right?" Jolene touched her shoulder.

"I think so."

"I hope no one was seriously hurt."

"Or killed," Big Al echoed.

They all watched while the paramedics tended to the injured.

Big Al fidgeted. Finally, unable to take it any longer, he grabbed the arm of a silver-haired officer. "Theodore? Any casualties?"

"Not that we know of." The older man's face looked grim. "We haven't found anyone dead yet, but a hell of a lot of people are injured." He strode off, responding to a call from inside.

Anniversary's lone ambulance, already gone with Colton, wasn't enough to handle all the people needing medical attention. Another ambulance was called in from Athens, one more from Carthage, and several private citizens volunteered their vehicles. As far as she could tell, none of the injuries, miraculously enough, appeared life-threatening, though Jewel was positive she'd seen several broken limbs.

"What about the driver of the car?" Jolene wondered out loud. "I wonder who it is, and how the hell he was going that fast in the parking lot to come clean through the building."

The driver of the car...Jewel froze. Though she'd managed to avoid thinking about it, she had no choice but to connect the dots. She knew why the car had smashed into the building. None of this would have happened if she hadn't been working there.

"I don't recognize that Buick." Al scratched his head. "Texas tags, but it must be from out of town. I'm thinking it was some tourist who had too much to drink."

"See if they've found the driver," Jewel urged. "Or I will."

Something in her tone made Al look hard at her. "Are you sure you're all right?"

"I'm sure. I just want to see who did this."

"Yeah, me, too." Without another word, he took off to talk with the police clustered in groups outside the unsafe and unstable building.

He returned a few minutes later. "They haven't found the driver. No one was inside the vehicle. But that car was reported stolen in Houston two days ago."

"Maybe the driver got out." As if sensing Jewel's unease, Jolene moved closer. "For all we know, he might be one of the hurt ones they transported to Athens."

"Maybe." But Jewel knew the driver would never be found. He'd probably rigged the gas pedal, and hadn't even been in the Buick when it hit. The car had been meant to send another message. Though apparently he wasn't ready to kill her yet, Leo wasn't above hurting those she cared about to make her suffer.

Cared about? She drew a sharp breath, the truth slamming into her. She cared about Colton. A lot.

"Jewel?" Big Al stared at her. "You're not about to faint or something, are you?"

Startled, she raised her face. "No. I'm just horrified, that's all."

He shifted his feet uneasily. "You were looking kind of...dangerous, or something." He laughed without a trace of humor. "Like this car crash was personal, or you planned on a vendetta."

If only he knew how accurate his statement was.

"Personal?" Her laugh matched his. "Colton was hurt." She looked over her shoulder at Jolene. "I'd really like to go see him and make sure he's okay."

Al's round face cleared. "That's what you were thinking about. Colton. I guess I was being paranoid."

She jerked her head in a nod, unable to tell him that actually, he'd been dead-on correct. This entire incident was personal. Leo's people again.

"We'll go in a minute, okay?" Jolene chewed her fingernail.

Jewel nodded. She scanned the crowd of gawkers the police were keeping contained behind yellow crime-scene tape. The hired killer could be any of them. She had no way of knowing.

Pushing through her dazed co-workers, she grabbed a uniformed officer's sleeve. "Excuse me, please. Was the driver of the car—?"

"We're still looking for him, ma'am."

"What about under? Have you checked to see if anyone was pinned under the car?"

Compassion darkened his expression as he patted her arm. "We're checking on that right now, miss. We've got people moving as much debris as they can. As long as the structure remains safe, we'll continue looking." He hurried away.

When Jewel would have followed him, Jolene grabbed her arm. "Come on, honey. I'll take you into Athens now to check on your man."

For a second, the words didn't register. "My..." Colton. She meant Colton. "I'd like to know about the driver."

Gently, Jolene steered her away. "That driver is long gone. For somebody to do something like that, he had to be drinking. A guy like that won't want to be found."

Because she was right, Jewel let the other waitress lead her away, toward the parking lot.

"How badly was Colton hurt?"

Not wanting to seem ungrateful, Jewel tried to focus on Jolene's face. "He was unconscious, but they didn't seem overly concerned."

"Good."

The drive to the hospital passed in an early morning blur. With sunrise still hours away, their headlights cut a path through curving road and wilderness. Jolene chattered nonstop with Jewel managing to nod at all the appropriate places.

East Texas Medical Center looked all too familiar. Her wolf recoiled and Jewel shuddered.

Jolene noticed. "Honey, I hope you're not in shock."

"I'm not." As soon as they'd parked under a light post, Jewel climbed out of the car. "Come on."

"Slow down." Jolene hurried to catch up. "It's still dark and no one else is around. We need to stay together."

"You're right." Jewel slowed her pace, so the older woman could keep up. "I'm sorry, I'm so worried about Colton."

When they entering the brightly lit deserted lobby, the temperature dropped twenty degrees.

"Why are hospitals always so cold?" Jolene complained.

"We're here to check on Colton Reynolds."

The woman at the front desk smiled at their inquiry. "Let me see." She punched his name into her computer. "You ladies are in luck. Looks like they just moved him from intensive care to a room on this floor. His room will be that way." She gave them directions.

Moving silently down deserted well-lit hallways, they turned corner after corner without encountering a single person.

"I feel like a rat in a maze." Arms wrapped around herself, Jolene looked uncomfortable. "I've never liked hospitals."

"Me either," Jewel admitted. "Here we are."

The door was partially open. Jewel pushed inside, glad to see the room was lit.

Colton was sitting up in bed.

"Shouldn't you be asleep?" she chided. "It's four-thirty in the morning."

"Jewel." His look seared her, even across the room. His face was bruised, but the only thing bandaged was his right arm. "I was worried about you."

Unable to speak for the tightness in her throat, Jewel nodded.

"She was worried about you, too, mister." Jolene wrapped her arm around Jewel's shoulders.

"We thought she might go after that Buick's driver with her bare hands."

Because the other waitress was uncomfortably close, Jewel moved away from her, toward the bed. Toward Colton.

He held out his good arm.

She moved into him, struck by the oddest urge to weep.

"Shhh," he murmured, smoothing her hair away from her forehead, as if he knew.

From the doorway, Jolene made a sound of approval.

Jewel didn't care. "What happened to you? Is your arm broken?"

"No." He lifted the bandage. "I had some cuts and bruises. That's all. I was lucky. The table blocked me from serious injury."

"I thought you were…" She couldn't finish. Clearing her throat, she tried again, reaching for the utterly banal. "I'm so glad you're all right."

Frowning, Jolene shook her head. "Tell him how you really feel."

Both Colton and Jewel gave her identical looks.

"I am glad he's all right," Jewel repeated.

"Okaaaay." Jolene threw up her hands. "I'll shut up now."

Colton ignored her. "I want out of here."

Jewel pulled back, remembering how he'd helped her leave this same hospital when she'd felt the same. "Are you sure you should?"

"I'm fine. They already told me. I have a mild concussion, nothing more."

Unable to stop touching him, she glanced over her shoulder at Jolene, still standing in the doorway watching. "I had to get a ride…"

"I can take you home." Jolene shrugged, grinning. "It does my heart good to see the two of you. It's been so long since I've been around two people in love." She waved away Jewel's attempt to protest. "I know when I'm not wanted. I'll wait out here in the waiting room. You two take your time. I saw a new copy of *People* magazine I want to read." She bustled away.

Feeling her cheeks heat, Jewel turned back toward Colton. "This is my fault. Leo hurt you and destroyed the restaurant just to get to me."

"Maybe." He planted a fierce kiss on her mouth, stunning her. "Or maybe not. Accidents do happen, you know. It might have simply been some drunken idiot, ramming into the building because he hit the accelerator instead of the brake."

Desire flared. Completely inappropriate and, even more shocking, without her having gone through a failed change first. This so stunned her, she bit off the comment she'd been about to make.

"Did they ever find the driver?" Colton's question brought her back to reality.

"No. They never found him," she said quietly, pulling away. "Why don't you get dressed, and we'll let Jolene take us home?" Without waiting to hear his answer, she took off for the waiting area. Instinctively, she reached for her silver wolf necklace, the one she never removed. It was gone.

That necklace had been the one thing Leo couldn't take from her, and now he had. She must have lost it in the confusion at work.

If there was a way to get it back, she vowed, she would.

An hour after Jolene dropped them off at Colton's place, the urge to change nearly brought Jewel to her knees. Tired of confinement, her wolf alter ego wanted freedom. Jewel couldn't say she blamed it.

She had to try to change. With Colton settled in his bed, dozing, and the pending dawn's rosy glow quickly chasing away the shadows and darkness, she knew she'd not have a better opportunity.

Slipping from the house into the backyard, she stood still, fully human, and sniffed the air like an animal. Her nostrils flared as she took in the myriad scents—lake and fish and damp grass.

No men, no other humans. Thanks to Colton's

tree-shaded lakeside acreage, she was safe, for now. With anticipation coiled low in her belly, she strode to the little copse of trees at the water's edge and, leaving her sundress on this time, dropped to the ground. On all fours, she crouched, letting the feel of the earth seep into her. Inhaling through her mouth, she tried to slow her racing heartbeat, wanting calm before the utter chaos of change overtook her.

Relaxing in increments, her confidence soared. Unlike the other times when she'd attempted this, something felt…right. Clicked. Now, maybe she could—

"Jewel?"

Colton's voice. She jerked her head up. Inside, her wolf-self bared her teeth and snarled.

Damn it. A quick glance at the ever-lightening sky showed dawn was imminent.

"Jewel? Where are you?"

"Right here." Jumping to her feet and hurrying barefoot across the grass toward the house, she quickly brushed leaves and dirt from her dress. "What are you doing out of bed? You should be resting." Though she tried, she couldn't manage to keep the edge from her voice.

"I was." He ran a hand through his hair, his gaze searching her face in the glow from his porch light. "But something woke me, I'm not sure what. Are you all right?"

She had to get him back to bed. Her body still hummed with the need—no, the *compulsion*—to change. "I'm fine. Just getting a little air." Reaching for his arm, she drew back, not daring to touch him while she was in this state. "Come on, let's get you back to bed."

"What's wrong?" He didn't move. "You sound...different."

Shifting her weight from foot to foot, she inhaled deeply. Any minute now, her fragile control would shatter. "Nothing's wrong." Swallowing past the lie, she forced a smile, shaking her head when she saw the disbelief in his shadowed eyes. "I don't feel well," she admitted. "I thought a bite of air might help."

"A *what?*"

"Bit. A bit of air."

"Did it?"

She started to reply, then a sharp pain stabbed her abdomen. Gasping, she doubled over.

"Jewel? Are you all right?" He reached for her arm. She dodged him before he could touch her. As she did, the wolf broke free.

"Get back," she gasped. Dropping, she belly-crawled out of the porch light, hoping to reach the edge of the trees, where darkness was deeper. "Go inside the house."

"Jewel?" He wasn't listening. Instead, she heard his footsteps as he moved toward her.

Crap. Her body stretched, convulsing her. Her bones began to lengthen, sending pain shooting through her. Pain wasn't good, though this felt…better. Closer.

Feeling her wolf's rage, she writhed on the ground. Letting a human see this was against the most basic of Pack laws.

Convulsing again, she clawed at the ground. Her paws raked at the grass, tearing through to damp earth. This time, the change *was* coming, she could feel it. No time to worry about him or Pack law, not now. She knew she must only concentrate on changing, if she wanted to stay alive.

Confined far too long, her wolf-self broke free with a vengeance. Rejoicing, she let the beast come, hoping, praying nothing would go wrong.

Then Colton touched her.

"Noooooo!" she screamed, part howl. "Get back."

But he wouldn't listen. No doubt he thought she was dying. "Jewel, hang on. Let me carry you into the house and I'll call 911. I left my cell there."

He scooped her up close, pinning her arms to her sides.

Still, she fought him. With teeth and claws and everything wild that would not be denied. "Let me go."

"Shhh," he attempted to soothe her, trying to hang on to her while she lashed out and struggled to get away.

Could he not see what she was becoming? Did he not feel her silken pelt erupting on smooth skin?

Evidently not. At five feet eight inches and a hundred and twenty pounds, she was no match for his six-feet-plus height and muscle. She could feel her bones sliding back into place, and the edges of her vision blurred as wolf acquiesced to human form.

She was going to pass out. Needing all of her strength to remain conscious, she stopped struggling.

"Let me get you into the house. You'll be all right, I promise." Obviously believing this was some sort of seizure, he continued murmuring. When they reached the kitchen door, he turned the knob with one hand, kicked it open and carried her to the sofa.

Gently, he placed her on the worn cushions, sliding his arms out from under her. Desire slammed into her, blazing fire through her veins. As he straightened to move away, she grabbed him.

"Wait. Don't go." Out of control, she pulled him down and kissed him. The feel of his mouth opening under hers was like adding gasoline to an inferno.

She felt the catch of his breath as he returned her kiss. Triumph, heady and compelling, fueled her need. Now, she would have him now, wrapped around her, buried deep inside her.

Using her hand, she tore at his clothing.

"No." He ripped his mouth away. Chest rising and falling rapidly, he straightened, glaring at her with desire still dark in his eyes.

Unable to help herself, she writhed on the sofa, her hand where his body should be.

"Stop it." His sharp order sounded like rusty nails, and she laughed, taunting him.

"You want me, I know. I can see." Lifting her dress, she moved her hips, mimicking the motion of sex. "I'm wet, I'm ready." She reached out, meaning to stroke the huge bulge in the front of his pants.

Instead, he captured her hand. "Jewel, stop." He sounded as if he was gritting his teeth.

"I can't," she cried, giving him honesty, her need pushing away everything else. "Please, Colton. Please."

Their gazes caught, held. For the space of one heartbeat she thought he might give in to what they both wanted.

Instead, he shook his head. "Not until you tell me what's going on."

"I…can't. That's the truth." A single tear rolled down her cheek, startling her.

Colton walked to his truck. He drove off in a screech of tires, leaving her alone with her desire and her pain, a caged wild animal, unable to break free.

Chapter 10

Two nights' tips weren't enough to bankroll an ant. If she was going to flee again, she'd need a lot more than that. Big Al had called that morning, explaining he was calling all his employees to warn them it would be weeks, maybe months before he was able to operate. Like all the other former employees of Jack's Grill on the Water, Jewel once again put on a skirt and a short-sleeved blouse and hit the pavement in search of another job.

She left Colton asleep and headed into town in the relatively cool morning. Still, by the time she'd walked the distance, her light cotton blouse was plastered to her back.

Still, she went from one restaurant to another, filling out applications and participating in cursory interviews.

No one was interested in hiring her. Finally, the manager at the local Burger Barn told her why. "Trouble seems to follow you," he said. "Your house burned, then Jack's Grill was wrecked. No one wants to take a chance they'll be next."

She might as well have worn a big scarlet letter on her forehead, maybe a *T* for *trouble* or a *C* for *cursed.*

Outside, the sun beamed brightly, birds sang in the trees, and weekenders, as the locals called the city dwellers who came down to spend the weekend in their lake houses, strolled the streets in brightly colored shorts and sandals. In the few hours she'd spent looking, the heat had climbed, approaching triple digits.

A typical summer day in a lake town. She eyed a laughing family of five eating ice-cream cones and wondered what the hell she was going to do.

For now, she'd better head back to Colton's before the thermometer showed one hundred.

In preparation, she bought a diet soda with lots of ice. If she kept to the shade, the long walk might not be too bad. She could always jump in the lake to cool off.

"Jewel! Wait up."

Jewel turned, the sun blinding her. "Reba?"

Shading her eyes with her hand, she watched as the other woman hurried across the parking lot.

"It's so hot, even breathing is painful. What are you doing outside on a day like this?" Short of breath, Reba fanned herself. She wore an orange pair of cotton capris and a yellow, green and orange patterned tank top.

"Trying to find another job." Jewel took a long drink and shrugged. "I'm not having much luck. They all seem to think I'm jinxed."

"Ah, honey let all the fuss die down. After a week or two goes by, they'll forget all about it."

"I don't have a week or two."

Reba frowned. "I don't know what you mean, but you may be right. I was looking for you. We've got to talk. Remember what I told you last night? About Colton?"

Squinting at the other woman, Jewel nodded. The sun beat down unmercifully. Beads of perspiration ran down Jewel's back. "Please. Not this again. I have enough problems."

"I *knew* you didn't believe me," Reba crowed.

Then sobering, she waggled her finger at Jewel. "But you will now. There's someone I'd like you to meet."

"Is this person willing to hire me?"

"Not hardly."

"Then why do I want to meet him? I wasn't kidding when I said this isn't a good time." Moving into the limited shade offered by a spindly oak tree, Jewel thought she might throw up. The heat was unbelievable.

"Not him, her. And believe me, you'll want to meet her."

"Right now, all I want is a cold shower and some iced tea."

"Jewel," Reba's no-nonsense tone matched the gleam in her eye. "You have to meet her."

With a sigh, Jewel drained the last of her drink. "Okay, I'll bite. Why?"

"Remember what I told you about Colton?"

"That he's abusive? Yes, I do. And I've seen no evidence that would make me ever believe that of him."

"You know what?" Reba shook her head, her eyes sad. "I thought the same thing until the man I've been seeing introduced me to Bettina. You really need to meet her."

"You still haven't told me why."

Taking a deep breath, Reba drew herself up and

exhaled. "Because…" She swallowed. "She's Colton's girlfriend."

"Colton has a *girlfriend?*" Every nerve in Jewel's body went quiet. Utterly still, the kind of motionless waiting her wolf adopted right before bringing down a deer.

"Had. He had a girlfriend. I knew you didn't know." Reba sighed again. "And I can tell from your expression that the news shocks you."

"Yes, it does. But I really don't want to meet Colton's former girlfriend. What will that prove?"

"You will." Reba grabbed her arm. "Come on. She's waiting in my office. I'll drive."

"I don't know."

"No more beating around the bush." Sniffing, Reba wiped away a tear. "Bettina's all beat-up. She's been abused, Jewel. Horribly. By Colton. She wants to talk to you. Once you see what he did to her, you'll see why I'm so upset. You won't want to have anything else to do with Colton Reynolds, ever."

Jewel's past rushed up to meet her. Images of Leo, his big, meaty fist pummeling her stomach, made Jewel wince. Her stomach dropped. "Not Colton."

"Yes, Colton. I've been trying to warn you."

If Reba had wanted to push a hot button, she'd

found one. Despite the scorching sun, Jewel couldn't move. All she could think was *not Colton.*

Not again. Good Lord, not again.

She'd been in this Bettina's shoes. No one had believed her either. The one time she'd summoned up enough courage to call the police, the cops had joked around with Leo, saying next time to hit her in places where the bruises didn't show.

She'd learned her lesson. No matter what he'd done to her after that, Jewel had never called the police again.

She couldn't even contact the Pack shaman, Luc Harrick, her spiritual leader. She'd been afraid he'd tell Leo. After all, he was one of them, just like the police had been. Despite his supposed vow of silence, when push came to shove, she'd bet he'd cave. They all did.

Pack was Pack. They banded together, took care of their own. Though Jewel was technically one of them, thanks to Leo, she'd become an outsider. Now, on the run, she felt like an outcast also.

"Reba, I still can't believe Colton's behind whatever this woman says he did. I'm very, very skeptical."

Expression grim, Reba nodded, her long earrings swinging wildly. "I was, too, until I heard her story. Jewel, Bettina knew Colton before he moved here. She told me Colton seduced her while he was still married. Between the affair and the abuse, she couldn't take it. She started using drugs."

"Have you talked to Colton?"

"I'd planned on talking to him, but Bettina begged me not to. She's afraid he'll come after her again."

Despite the tremor that ripped through her at the memories those words evoked, Jewel crossed her arms. "Talk to him. That woman may be lying."

"Why would she do that?" Despite the question, Reba looked hopeful.

"Maybe she has a personal vendetta. Maybe she went out with him once and when nothing happened, she couldn't accept it. Maybe—"

"Jewel, stop. She has a witness. I told you I've been seeing a man. He backed her up. He used to be a friend of Colton's. He swears what Bettina said is true."

Shaken, Jewel rocked back on her heels. "Who is he? What's his name?"

"Roy Mansfield. He works in Houston at Channel Four. He's a very reputable person."

"I'll go with you," Jewel said.

Nodding, Reba led the way. She drove a shiny red Mustang. Jewel climbed in and buckled her seat belt. Neither woman spoke while they navigated the tourist traffic on Main Street. A few minutes later, they turned into the small office complex where Reba ran her business and parked. Jewel had been here once before, when she'd signed her lease.

"Come on." Jangling her keys, Reba hurried ahead. Skin prickling, Jewel couldn't help but scent the air. She smelled nothing but exhaust and the hamburger place down the street. Ordinary.

Still, she couldn't shake the niggling worry in the back of her mind.

Inside, Reba nodded at the receptionist and turned down a hall. "My office is near the back."

The ornate oak door was closed. "Are you ready?" Reba looked at Jewel.

Throat tight, Jewel nodded.

Reba opened the door. "Here we are. This is Bettina. Bettina, meet Jewel."

From behind, the other woman appeared normal. Thick, sable-colored hair fell past her shoulders. She had a trim figure, and olive-toned skin. But when she turned to face them, Jewel couldn't stifle her gasp.

Bettina looked as though she'd come out of a losing bout in the boxing ring.

"I know," Bettina said, trying to chuckle and merely making an odd, clucking sound. Her lip was split open and the dark bruise around her swollen-shut left eye could only have been caused by a fist. "I'm lucky, I guess."

"Lucky?" Outraged and horrified, Jewel tried to keep her voice down. "How can you say such a thing?"

"No broken bones." Bettina shrugged, wincing. "Or, at least I don't think I have any."

Looking at Bettina was like looking into a mirror of her former life. "Have you been checked out by a doctor?"

"No."

"Not yet," Reba interjected. "I'm trying to convince her to let me run her over to Athens to the hospital."

"We'll see." Bettina sounded noncommittal. "So you're the one Reba told me about."

"What did Reba tell you?"

"That you're living with Colton."

"Staying with him. There's a difference. We're not involved."

Bettina's huge brown eyes went from Jewel to Reba, then back again. "If that's true, that's good."

"It is." Voice firm, Jewel squelched her instinctive horror and sympathy for the other woman. "And let me ask you one more time, so I'm clear on this. You're telling me Colton Reynolds did this to you?"

"Yes."

One simple word, but enough to shatter everything Jewel had believed she knew.

"When?"

"Last night."

After he'd refused her attempt to seduce him and driven away, fast and furious.

Still, despite all the evidence to the contrary, fool that she was, Jewel couldn't make herself believe. "Did you go to the police?"

For the first time, Bettina looked away. Instead of answering, she hung her head.

Again, the skin on the back of Jewel's neck prickled. "Bettina, did you?"

Reba made a sound of distress, but Jewel ignored her. "Answer me, please."

"No. No police. I…couldn't." Her voice faint, she sounded about to weep.

"Why not?" Though she herself had done the same thing, too many times to count over the course of her marriage to Leo, this woman didn't even live in the same town. Any repercussions she might suffer seemed far outweighed by bringing her abuser to justice.

"I just couldn't. I love…loved him."

There had to be a better reason than that. Jewel knew all about that kind of inner turmoil. She softened her voice. "Didn't you want to stop him from doing it again to another woman?"

"Yes." Bettina raised her head, brown eyes swimming with tears. "That's why I'm here, talking to you. Reba says you're her friend, that you've been through a lot. I don't want to hear about another victim to his craziness."

Colton? Part of Jewel wanted to howl. The other part, the savage, wild part, wanted to attack him with claws and teeth. She took a deep breath, trying for calm. This wasn't her small town in upstate New York. The police here wouldn't automatically take the man's side. Would they? "Call the police. Report him. Do it now, before your bruises fade."

"No." Bettina's voice went sharp. She looked from Jewel to Reba, her puffy eyes narrowed to slits. "You said I only had to talk to her. You didn't say nothin' about talking to the police."

Reba nodded. "Jewel, please. Give her a break."

"I don't understand. Why not report him? Why not get him locked up?"

Wiping her nose with the back of her hand, Bettina sniffled. "He threatened to kill me if I did. You might not be so lucky. He might not even give you a choice."

Shoulders hunched, she began crying in earnest. Instantly, Reba enfolded her in her arms, shooting Jewel a meaningful look over the other woman's back.

"See what I mean?" she mouthed.

"And the time before last night? How long ago was that?" Not bothering to disguise her rage, Jewel stared at Bettina's bowed head, waiting to hear her response.

But Bettina was crying too hard to answer.

Reba answered for her. "She told me the last time they made love was three days ago."

The day of the fire. Sickened, unable to press the issue any longer, Jewel turned to go. She needed some time alone to try and reconcile this woman's accusations with the man she'd come to know and trust.

And believe in.

"Wait!" Bettina raised her tear-streaked face. "Right now you're probably thinking I'm crazy. You're thinking Colton is the kindest, most even-tempered man you've ever met." She sniffled. "He was like that with me, too. At first."

Like Leo. Leo had disguised his true nature until the marriage ceremony was over and he had his new bride alone in their bedroom.

Blood running cold, Jewel couldn't keep herself from asking. "What changed him?"

"Sex." Bettina swallowed, lifting her chin. "Just

don't have sex with him. He likes it rough and hard. That's when he'll hurt you the first time, that's when he'll draw blood."

Jewel stared. Leo had used that excuse beyond reasonable bounds. The first time they'd made love, he'd cut her. The second, she'd suffered broken ribs, the third, a broken arm, and lost a tooth. After less than a week, she'd known he meant to torture her until she begged for death, all in the guise of love.

How had she managed to find two violent men? Even here, in the Texas countryside, she'd managed to prove her judgment would never be good.

"I've got to go." Lifting her hand in a half-hearted wave, she couldn't meet Reba's gaze. Instead, she focused on the other woman, trying to understand. "Thanks for warning me. Take care of yourself, Bettina."

Bettina lifted a tearstained face to give her a watery smile. "You, too. And Jewel, please don't tell him you've met me. I don't want him coming back to finish what he started."

On the long walk home, Jewel tried to come up with a plan. She had to leave. Mentally, she counted the money she'd been able to save. She had roughly $265. Not enough to buy a car, though she could purchase a one-way ticket on a red-eye to LaGuardia. She wouldn't need a car in New

York and the huge city would swallow her, giving her precious anonymity.

It was a good plan, except for one thing. New York City was crawling with Leo's associates.

She'd have to reverse direction. Go west. Or south.

Thinking of the South made her think of Colton, with his slow drawl and bedroom eyes. Colton, who like Leo, wore two faces, beautiful on the outside, but rotten at the core.

Just don't have sex with him. God alone knew how close she'd come.

God and her wolf.

At the thought, her inner beast snarled.

Colton had awakened to sunlight streaming through the windows and an empty house. Wandering into the kitchen, he found a fresh pot of coffee and a note. Jewel had gone into town to look for a job. Squinting, he reread her signature line. She'd even written the time she'd left—eleven. It was now two. She'd been gone three hours.

He pictured her walking to town, unprotected, and his blood ran cold. By choice he lived in one of the more remote areas of the lake, and the winding roads and wild forests provided ample opportunity for someone to get her, or shoot at her, or...

Snatching his car keys off the dresser, he stepped into a pair of shorts, dropped a T-shirt over his head and hurried for his truck.

He'd find her and bring her home.

Rounding the curve that led out of his subdivision, he noticed the traffic seemed unusually light, but then he remembered the tourists usually went home on Sundays.

A sniper wouldn't try for her unless he had a clear shot.

Colton saw the car before he saw her. Driving way too fast, the white Cadillac Eldorado appeared aimed like a bullet at a figure walking on the side of the road.

Jewel!

He gunned his truck, moving over to the wrong side of the road to shield her.

She looked up. Saw him and the other vehicle bearing down on her.

Moving fast, she leaped for the trees.

The Caddy swerved, missing Colton by inches.

Bouncing over ruts, the truck tried to flip. Muscles screaming, Colton held on, praying he could maintain control. When he finally brought the pickup to a shuddering halt, there was no sign of the Cadillac.

Both the car—and Jewel—had disappeared.

He found her in a small thicket, shaking. When she saw him, she stepped out into a clearing, arms wrapped around her middle.

"They tried to hit me." Though she gasped for breath, she didn't sound surprised. But, despite her matter-of-fact tone, her nostrils flared and the whites of her eyes showed. Delayed terror?

When he reached to comfort her, she jerked away. "Don't touch me."

"What's wrong?" Deliberately, he kept his voice soft. Soothing.

"Nothing," she said, but she continued to watch him as if he were a venomous snake.

"Let me take you home."

Skirting a wide path around him, she stepped over the ruts in the grass left by his tires, climbed into his truck and buckled herself in.

When he got in beside her, she gave an involuntary jerk, though she looked out the window rather than at him.

"Are you all right?"

"Fine," she snapped. "Let's get out of here."

He started the engine, drove up the embankment, and back onto the road. For the first time since he'd met her, the silence between them felt uncomfortable. He couldn't put his finger on what, but something had changed.

Was it because of the way he'd surprised her outside in his yard earlier that morning?

Why not simply ask her?

"I want to talk to you about what happened this morning." Keeping an eye on the road, he also watched her for a reaction. Any reaction.

She gave none. "There's nothing to say." The flatness of her voice was as if she were talking to a stranger, not even a stranger she particularly liked.

"That's it." He pulled into his driveway and parked, leaving the engine idling. "What the hell is going on with you?"

"I don't want to talk about it." She set her chin and crossed her arms. "If you don't mind, I'd like to go inside."

"I do mind. I want to know what you were doing when you snuck out of the house before dawn."

"It's none of your business." Shoving her door open, she slammed it behind her and ran for the house.

He'd never seen a woman run so fast.

Moving much more slowly, he got out of his truck and locked the doors before pocketing the keys. The beginnings of a headache hovered at the back of his eyes and he blinked, willing it away.

She wasn't in the kitchen. Or the den, or the dining room. Suddenly, inexplicably weary, he trudged down the hall to her bedroom, finding the door closed.

"Jewel?" No answer. He knocked twice, then tried the handle, knowing the lock didn't work. As he opened the door, she spun around to face him.

"Leave me alone." Her lips drew back in a snarl.

"What's wrong with you?"

"Wrong with me?" Her tone rose. "Despite the fact that I completely misjudged you, not a whole lot. Unless you take into account the fact that Leo isn't going to rest until he drives me insane and has me bleeding and cowed. I don't have a job or money or any way to escape him. So do I start digging my grave and planning my funeral, or what?"

He wanted to hold her, to touch that silky short hair and soothe away the tension in her neck. Instead, he stayed where he was, unmoving. Her eyes, while flashing with anger, also were full of fear. "This really isn't about me, is it?"

"Get out." Toneless, she gave the order in a voice so low it sounded like a growl. "Get out and leave me alone."

Instead, he took a step forward.

She opened her mouth to speak, and convulsed instead. She made a howling sound, her expression stricken. "Oh, God. Not now!"

Heart pounding, instantly, he crossed to her side. "What is it, Jewel? What's wrong with you? Let me help."

"Get back," she snarled.

He reached for her. Dodging him, she dropped to the ground on all fours, facing him from that position, looking for all the world like an animal caught in a rusty trap.

"Jewel!"

"Go!" She convulsed again.

Was it his imagination, or was she suddenly surrounded by fireflies? He rubbed his eyes. Not fireflies, but sparkles of light, like an animated cartoon with magic. Pixie dust.

Was *he* on drugs? He couldn't be seeing this. Was her body changing shape? What the *hell* was going on here? Suddenly uncertain, he took a step back. Then another.

He'd just reached the doorway when she howled. The sound was so full of sadness, so full of pain, he couldn't leave.

The lights surrounding her intensified. Colors swirled, rainbows danced and sparkles flowed in random patterns.

Once, when he'd been young and stupid, he'd tried taking a hit of acid. He felt as if he were tripping on that right now.

He took a tentative step forward, half expecting to feel the ground tilt under his feet.

"Stay back," she warned from somewhere inside the maelstrom.

"Are you hurt?"

No answer. For a second he could have sworn he saw a wolf peering out at him. He blinked and the image had vanished.

As quickly as they'd begun, the colors and traces of light vanished.

Jewel lay on the floor, one arm flung out as if in entreaty, unconscious.

He crossed to her, lifting her wrist to check for a pulse.

The blood startled him. It seeped from her fingers, though he couldn't see any cuts.

As he watched, the trickle slowed, then stopped.

Jewel stirred. "Colton?" Her voice was thick, as though she'd just awakened from a deep sleep.

His first mistake was leaning close. When she kissed him, his second was deepening the kiss.

His body, always half-aroused around her, instantly sprung to life.

"I can't..." Swallowing, she pushed herself back, staring at him with desperate eyes.

This time, he kissed her. Like a man drowning, having denied himself far too long to continually resist. Her breathing shifted and she raised her hand, caressing his face. "Hounds help me, I need you."

Her words barely registered. Everything about her, the sleek, silky smoothness of her skin, the faint musk of her desire, trapped him as neatly as any spider with a web.

Desire slammed into him, tsunami strength, and he shuddered. He felt as if he were drowning, sinking slowly as the waves closed over him. He took a breath, trying for sanity, for air, all the while helplessly pushing himself against her.

"Are you…" He swallowed, tried again. "Are you sure?"

Instead of answering, she smiled. It was fierce, that smile, and full of secrets and desire. The power of that smile did him in.

Her hands were everywhere, her breath, soft upon his skin. But his need—oh, his need, it filled him, possessed him, and turned him into a wild thing.

She tore at his clothing. He heard the cloth rip and didn't care.

Her dress came off easily. At the sight of her, all curves and alabaster skin, he nearly lost control.

She drew him toward her.

Once again, he tried for restraint. "I don't want to hurt you," he rasped.

With a laugh, she climbed on top of him, her

tight femininity wrapping him in a silky cloak. She rode him, hard and fast and so furious he could no longer think. Only feel, only experience, and he knew in a flash of brilliance that it was her, only her. The one he should have waited for, the one he'd always want.

With a cry, he let loose. Opening his eyes, he saw a look in hers so conflicted, so full of desire and need and self-loathing, he nearly paused.

But he was too far gone to stop now and, as his essence poured into her, he could have sworn he heard a howl.

Chapter 11

The instant his body stopped quaking, she rolled off him, pushing him away when he reached out to hold her.

"No."

"Jewel, I—"

Pain and sadness mingled with fury in her expressive eyes.

"Thank you." She gave him a mocking smile, utterly false and breaking his heart. "We shouldn't have—"

"Don't." When he reached for her again, she

dodged, climbing from the bed to stand, arms crossed, glaring.

"I haven't been so thoroughly used since—"

Shoving himself up, he grabbed her and wrapped his arms around her. "Shhh. You know better than that."

"Do I?" She held herself stiffly, finally moving away. "I'm not sure who I hate most," she said. "Myself or you."

With that, she stalked off, not bothering to put on her clothes.

He followed. "What's wrong with you?"

"As if you didn't know."

"I *don't* know. We just made love and, as far as I can tell, both enjoyed it."

"Made love? Is that what you're calling it now?"

He sighed. "You know as well as I do that we've got something special between us."

"Do we?" One delicate brow arched. "I don't think so. That was lust. Raw lust. We scratched an itch. Nothing more. And I always feel like dirt afterwards."

He went still, searching her face. "Was that all this meant to you?"

"Does it ever mean anything else?" Her voice was bleak.

The tightness in his chest eased. "This isn't

your past, you know. This is your future." Aching
to hold her, he settled for reaching to tuck a strand
of wayward hair behind her ear. She flinched away
as if she thought he meant to hurt her, making him
bite back a curse.

"What did he do to you?"

She shook her head, her eyes bright with
unshed tears. "Don't touch me. Not right now."

"I won't." He kept his voice even, controlled,
showing no sign of the inner ache. "Jewel, if you
really feel that way, why'd you initiate it?"

"I had no choice."

"You always have a choice."

"Maybe you didn't listen." Her mouth a tight
line, she wouldn't meet his gaze. "I told you, I
can't control myself."

"Control what?"

"My need." Her laugh sounded hollow, bitter.
"Leo loved that about me. I swear he tried to make
me…"

"If Leo were here right now, I'd kill him."

"So would I."

He waited for her to finish. Then, when it
became apparent she had no plans to, he pushed.
"What happened there, on the floor of your room?
And out in the woods, before. Whatever happens
to you at those times? Whatever it is, it makes you

want to have sex, doesn't it? It was the same thing all those other times, wasn't it?"

Blanching, she jerked her head in a nod. "You've finally got it. I tried to tell you. Now are you happy? I've just given you something you can use to control me."

"Control you? I'm not Leo, remember." Holding himself utterly still, he willed her to look at him, to read his expression, to somehow discern the depth of his feelings for her.

She didn't.

"I don't want to control you."

"All men relish control. They thrive on it. You're no different."

"I'm not all men. No matter what, know this. What we just shared was more than sex, more than lust."

Now her brilliant green gaze flew to his. "Don't."

She reminded him of a furious, terrified bird with a badly broken wing. The question was could he heal her? Did he want to?

"Don't what?"

"Don't try to pretty it up. Call a spade a spade."

"I am. We have something between us. Something special. You know that."

"Special?" She snorted. "Even Leo didn't—"

"I told you, I'm not Leo," he roared, then

lowered his voice. "Don't compare me to that son of a bitch. Not ever again."

Gazes locked, they stared each other down. After a moment, she gave a slow nod. "You're right. I'm sorry."

"Apology accepted." He took a deep breath, knowing he must continue to push until she gave him the truth. "You're not ill, are you?"

"Not in the way you mean. But yes, I am."

Could she be any more ambiguous? This time he was having none of it. "Don't lie to me, Jewel. Not now."

"You're better off not knowing. Believe me."

How often in the past had he heard that? Though he knew both he and Jewel carried way too much baggage from their pasts, if he'd learned one thing from his experiences, he'd learned to despise lies.

"I want to know, damn it. I want the truth."

Silent, she pressed her lips together and said nothing.

His stomach knotted. He should have known better. That's what he got for thinking with the wrong part of his body. Taking a deep breath, he gave her one last chance.

"I'm trying to help you, Jewel. Is it too much to ask for you to respect me enough to tell me the truth?"

"Truth? You wouldn't know it if it bit you in the ass." Her voice vibrated with rage.

"What?"

"I met your girlfriend today, saw what you did to her. You're a monster." Her stone face crumpled. "And I had sex with you. What does that make me?"

"Girlfriend?" Impatient, he shook his head. "I don't have a girlfriend. What the hell are you talking about?"

"Bettina?" Her furious glare scorched him. "Does the name ring a bell?"

"Not at all. Who's Bettina?"

She searched his face. "Either you're one of the most accomplished liars I've ever met, or you're serious."

Moving closer, he shook his head. "I don't know anyone named Bettina, nor do I have a girlfriend. I've been alone since my daughter died." He didn't understand where they were going with this, but sensed he should follow her lead. Eventually, they had to come to truth, when they hit the rock bottom.

He watched the emotions play across her face. First and foremost, he saw hope, before her features went blank as she shut her feelings down. She seemed to do that a lot, whenever she got something she didn't want to face.

"Whatever," she said, shrugging as if she didn't care.

She began to pace, her movements jerky, agitated.

He followed. "Explain, please. Where did you get this false information?"

"I met her."

"Met...Bettina?"

"Yes. Reba introduced me to her. She said I needed to know what kind of man I was living with."

He couldn't have been more astounded. "Reba? I've known her for years. She should know better than to believe this woman's story without checking with me first."

"Right now, Reba thinks you're a monster."

Words stuck in his throat. He'd done a lot of wrong things in his lifetime, made his own share of mistakes, but he'd never hurt anything or anyone smaller or weaker than himself. "Why wouldn't Reba come to me?"

"Something like this is a touchy issue," Jewel reminded him. "Especially when a woman is battered as badly as Bettina was."

Battered. He closed his eyes. "What about the police? Did she fill out a report? Of course she didn't. No one's notified me, or even asked me any questions."

"No." She watched him closely. "I asked her that too. She said she couldn't go to the police. She was afraid you might kill her."

"Kill her?" He shook his head. "I don't even know her."

"There's more. Your friend Roy backed Bettina up."

"Roy?" Dragging a hand through his hair, he tried to make sense of her words. "My former co-worker from Houston? That Roy? What's he got to do with any of this?"

"Remember I told you Reba was seeing someone?"

He nodded. "Roy?"

"Yes."

"I don't understand." He felt as if he'd been kicked in the gut. When she told him Roy had not only corroborated Bettina's story, but made accusations of infidelity during his marriage, Colton could barely hang on to his rapidly vanishing self-control.

Flipping open his cell phone, he paged through the stored numbers, looking for Reba's real estate office.

"What are you doing?"

"I'm calling Reba first, then Roy. I want to get this straightened out once and for all."

Clenching his teeth, he punched in the number. After a few rings, Reba's voice mail picked up. He left a terse message, then tried Roy. Again he got voice mail; again he left a message. Done, he closed his phone, the movement carefully controlled.

Eyes narrowed, Jewel crossed her arms. "You're seriously pissed, aren't you?"

"Of course I am. I've never hit a woman in my life."

The breath seemed to go out of her in a rush. "You know, I believe you."

Breathing deeply, he forced his teeth to unclench. He was absurdly grateful. "I don't understand. Why would anyone, especially a total stranger, then a guy I've known for years, accuse me of such a thing? What would they have to gain?"

She shook her head. "I don't know."

The thought occurred to them both at the same time.

"Me," Jewel said. "This has something to do with me."

"Someone wants to make you distrust me." Now it all made sense. "I'm your only ally. If they could turn you against me, once again you'd be on your own."

"Not *someone*. Quit talking about him as

though he's anonymous. It's Leo. Even in prison, he's keeping his promise to come after me."

Though it was the only thing that made sense, he still had to caution her. "But how? That's what we need to find out."

Though she nodded, he knew she was afraid. Not of him, thank God. He never wanted her to fear him. Ever. "I want to talk to Reba and Roy, face-to-face. Then you and I need to go confront this Bettina in person."

"I agree."

"Good." Frustration coiled low in his belly, he dialed Reba's number again, disconnecting when her voice mail came on. "Still no answer. I'm going to run by her place, see if she's there."

"I don't know if that's such a good idea." For a moment, she appeared about to say something else.

"I do." Frustrated, Colton shoved his hand through his hair. "Come with me."

She appeared torn. "I… No. I'm actually not feeling too well. I'll wait here."

"Reba or no Reba, I've got to check in at the office." Quietly, he watched her. If she meant to leave, he could do nothing to stop her. "I'll be gone a couple of hours. We'll talk again when I get back."

If she was still there.

On the way to town, he cruised by Reba's

house, just in case. Her Mustang wasn't parked in the driveway, nor was it at the real-estate building.

He drove on in to work.

Once inside the newspaper office, Colton tried to call Reba again. Again, her voice mail picked up. This time, he left another message and organized his desk, pretended to be working on his story about Jewel. If he published it, he knew she'd never forgive him, but if he didn't, Floyd would have a fit. Either way didn't look good.

Right now he didn't much care. He wanted to find Reba and to confront this Bettina person. A woman he'd never even met, making such accusations, had better have a damn good reason.

And then Roy. That rankled even more. The man had just offered him a job, for Chrissakes.

To distract himself, he tried to focus on the job he'd been asked to do. Write the story. About Jewel. Maybe if he could find a different angle, do more research. For example, he'd like to find out what those sparkly lights surrounding her had been.

Psychic phenomena? He kicked back in his chair, hands behind his head, and tried to come up with an explanation.

But all he could think of was Jewel, and how well they'd fit together. He felt like a lovesick fool, obsessed with the wrong woman. Again.

"Colt!" Floyd came running, his large stomach bouncing. "Have you heard the news? How quickly can you have your story ready?"

"News?" Colton blinked. "What news? Which story?"

"The big story, the one on Jewel. Look what just came over the wire!" Floyd shoved a crumpled piece of paper under Colton's nose.

Colton read it once, heart sinking. He read it again, and pushed back his chair so hard it crashed into the wall behind him. Crap.

"Here." He tossed the paper back at Floyd. "I've got to go."

"Go?" Floyd goggled at him. "Hell, no. You'll stay and write your story. This is perfect timing. We'll sell a ton of papers. Get busy finishing it up. I'm putting it on the front page."

But Colton ignored him. He ran for the parking lot, keys in hand. He had to warn Jewel, see what she wanted to do.

Leo was out. He'd escaped from prison the night before. Despite a massive manhunt, he hadn't yet been found.

"Out? Are you sure?" Jewel dragged her hand through her disheveled hair for the tenth time. She paced, her long-legged stride eating up the distance quickly, before she pivoted and headed back toward him. Leo's escape had taken precedence over their other issues, now temporarily tabled by mutual silent agreement.

They were in Colton's kitchen, with the bright sunlight streaming in from the window, and the lake sparkling with dancing whitecaps.

A perfect summer day, if one wanted to fish or ski. A day to enjoy, if one's powerful and psychotic ex-husband weren't on the loose.

"Are you really sure?" Jewel asked again.

"Positive. The news release came over the wire from the AP." He snatched the remote from the countertop and punched the television on. "I'm sure it's all over the news."

And it was. Special broadcast. Updates every hour. No, Leo Licciardoni had not been caught. Both federal and state police were looking for him. All the New York and surrounding airports had been locked down and they were watching both the highways leaving the state and the ports.

"Authorities feel confident he will be caught quickly and returned to prison," the newscaster said.

A pounding on the door made them both jump.

"What the—?" He and Jewel exchanged startled glances.

Hand to her throat, she shook her head. "Leo wouldn't knock."

"I know." Still, he crossed the room quietly, checking through the peephole. What he saw stunned him, though he shouldn't have been surprised.

"Who is it?" Jewel stopped her pacing long enough to stare.

"There are five, maybe six news vans outside. I should have seen this coming."

She groaned. "They all know Leo swore to kill me. They're probably hoping to capture the event on live TV."

He didn't laugh at her joke. She was more accurate than she realized.

"What I don't understand is why the police aren't here offering protection."

Her rueful smile was tinged with a hint of fear. "I ditched the Federal Witness Protection people. They only offer help once. After that, you're on your own."

His cell phone rang. Checking the caller ID, Colton saw it was Floyd. No doubt furious and about to fire him.

He didn't answer.

"What am I going to do?" Jewel mused, almost to herself, still making her furious trek around his kitchen island, from the laundry room to the back door.

He shook his head, started to speak, took one look at her pinched and worried face and decided to go for it.

"We're leaving town," he said. "Now."

Eyes wide, she went still, reminding him of a wild animal caught in the headlights of an oncoming car. *"We?"*

"Yes. The two of us." He waved a hand, not daring to touch her, knowing he'd be lost if he did. "Grab whatever you want to take with you. There's no time to waste."

She stared at him, her eyes were huge and very, very green. "Why?"

He could think of several reasons. He could say none of them. "Let's just say guys like your ex-husband should never win."

After a moment's silence, she nodded, accepting his explanation, which told him how desperate she was. "Thank you. But where can we go?"

He thought for a moment. "My hunting lease."

"What?"

"I have a place I lease for hunting. It's northwest of here, close to Possum Kingdom Lake. It's accessible only by a single dirt road which winds up the bluff. You can see someone coming for miles."

She moved restlessly, pushing her hair back from her face. "I don't know."

"I do. There's no place better."

"I was thinking more like another country. Canada or—" she swallowed "—Mexico."

"They can hire guns there, too."

He grabbed her arm, feeling that shock zing through him as it always did when he touched her. "Come on. We can talk in the car."

"What about them?" She jerked her head toward the front yard. "How are we going to get away from them? We can't drive away—they'll follow us."

The only other way was by boat. But then what?

Theodore at the marina had been trying to sell his old Jeep for months.

"We'll take the boat." He felt a sense of right-ness flood him.

"And then what?"

He smiled. "Trust me. I've got a plan."

And it worked like a charm. They crept from the back of the house down to his boat dock. Using oars, he pushed out from the dock, down the channel, waiting until they'd reached the entrance of the main body of water before starting his motor.

The newshounds clustered out front of his house had no clue they were even gone.

At the marina, Colton tied up his boat in front of the restaurant and located Theodore reading the paper in the back. Handing over cash, Colton accepted the keys and the title to the Jeep.

"It's full of gas," Theodore offered, baring his yellow teeth. "You'll love it come deer season."

Since deer season was still four months away, Colton merely nodded. "I'll bet I will. Would you mind putting my boat in a slip for me while I'm gone? I'll settle up with you when I return."

"No problem." Theodore grinned. "Have fun."

They drove off in the Jeep, successfully leaving the newshounds camped out at Colton's place.

"I brought these." Digging in her tote, Jewel held up an ornate, hammered-metal case. It looked old and well taken care of. After opening the lid and checking the contents, Jewel slipped the case into her bag.

"Silver bullets." She gave him a tremulous smile. "Now I'm ready. Let's go."

They headed west.

Every half hour, his cell phone rang. After the fourth call from Floyd, Colton turned off the ringer.

Skirting the southern edge of the Dallas/Fort Worth Metroplex, they drove west. Eventually the concrete and freeways gave way to small towns and two-lane roads. Some were little more than a few shacks. In the distance, mesas rose treeless from the prairie.

Jewel sat up straight, watching their surroundings. "This is different."

"Welcome to West Texas."

"What happened to the trees? They're so...small." She reached for her neck, then stopped. He'd noticed the movement before. Turning onto the road leading to his leased land, he let the car coast to a stop. "What's wrong?"

"I had a necklace I always wore. I never took it off. It was unusual, a silver wolf. I lost it when the car crashed into the restaurant."

"I'll buy you another."

Her emerald eyes widened. "Colton—"

Because he didn't know what had prompted his rash promise, he did what he'd been wanting to do since he'd seen her nearly run down by the car. He kissed her. Hard.

She made a startled sound, low in her throat. Then, with a soft sigh, she kissed him back.

He deepened the kiss. As always, desire flared to life. But they were in an open-sided Jeep, parked on the side of the road.

Breaking away, he grinned at her, all the while marveling at the strength of his own arousal. He'd never felt anything like he felt with her, hot and consuming, searing yet safe.

Tentatively, she smiled back. "What's so funny?"

"I'm just happy. This is the first time you've kissed me without it being after one of your episodes."

"Hmmm." She looked thoughtful. "I think you're right."

"I know I am." He wanted to press her, ask her what she thought this new development might mean, but knew better. Instead, he put the Jeep into gear and pulled back onto the road.

They went miles before they saw another car passing acres and acres of rolling farmland, dotted with the occasional mesquite tree and odd herd of cattle.

"Where *are* we?" she asked, a slight frown crinkling her brow. "Are we still in Texas? Never mind another state, this looks like another planet."

He laughed. "I like West Texas. All wide open sky and room to run."

"It's different. It makes me feel smaller, somehow."

"When I was small, my dad used to bring me out here. I'd pretend I was a wild animal or bird, deer or hawk or mountain lion, and wonder what it'd be like to have unfettered freedom."

"It's wonderful."

At his startled look, she bit her lip.

"I would imagine," she amended.

"Here we are." Slowing, he turned off the road. "We'll be glad to have the Jeep now. You'd better hold on." The dirt path to his deer lease wound up one hill and down another. Rocks and dirt warred with potholes and ruts. The Jeep bounced valiantly. He was glad the seat belts worked, holding them in place.

"Some people do this for fun," he told her.

She raised a brow. "What, they like to make their teeth rattle?"

"Yes. It's even better when you do this in the mud. Mudding, we call it."

Instead of answering, she shook her head.

A huge hawk screeched in the sky above them, diving into the tall grass for prey. Watching intently, Jewel licked her lips, her eyes blazing green.

"How I envy that bird."

"That's what I was talking about. You do understand, don't you?"

"Oh yes. You have no idea how much."

They continued on, over gully and ravine, up one embankment and down another.

"Where *is* this place?" she asked, hanging on to the panic bar on her side.

He tossed her a grin. "I told you, it's remote."

"That's the understatement of the year."

"The more remote, the better the hunting."

"Do you hunt here a lot?"

"In season, yes. The area's plentiful with game. Deer, wild pigs, turkey, you name it."

He could have sworn she licked her lips again.

Finally, they pulled into a clearing. "Here we are." The place looked exactly as it had the last time he'd been here. Not much. A weathered mobile home sat rusting in the sunlight.

"We should have the place to ourselves," he said, killing the engine. "Deer season is still months away. Though you can hunt pigs any time, not too many hunters come here in the heat of summer."

She nodded, her gaze on the mobile home. He couldn't tell from her expression whether she was appalled or approved. "This is yours?"

"I don't own it, no. The trailer house comes with the lease. I've got the place for five years."

Unlocking the door, he stepped inside and flicked on the lights. "Wait here. Let me get the windows open to let out some of the heat. It's like a furnace in here."

He left her outside, hoping she'd find some-thing to admire in the primitive beauty of the landscape. As he opened the windows he saw buzzards circling in the sky above them.

A bad omen? Or merely a dead animal?

Once a breeze was blowing through the trailer, the heat level dropped tremendously. He flicked on the two ceiling fans, then took a deep breath and went to get Jewel.

She was watching a small lizard sunning on a rock.

"It's still warm, but bearable now. And more than a little dusty." He wiped perspiration from his brow. "But it won't take long to get it cleaned up."

"Does the air conditioner work?"

"Sometimes." He gave her a rueful smile. "I turned it on, but the generator wasn't running. I'll try it again later. Come on in."

Stepping aside, he expected her to brush past him, to breeze around the place and inspect it, the way women do. Instead, she moved close and wrapped her arms around him.

His heart skipped a beat. "Jewel? What's up?"

She sighed. He felt the movement of her breasts like a caress. Chest to chest, she tilted her head to look at him, and gave a slow, sensual smile.

"Make love to me," she said.

At first, he wasn't sure he'd heard correctly,

though his swift and instant arousal belied his confusion. "Are you sure?"

She leaned into him, rubbing her body against his like a mischievous cat. "Positive."

He searched her face, his throat tight. "Jewel—"

"Just once, I want to make love to you without any compulsion." Voice tight, her expression was fierce. "Just once, I want to have sex because I want to. Because I desire you, need you." She kissed his chest at the collar of his shirt. "Crave you." She moved higher, to where the pulse beat at the base of his throat. "And long for you."

As he started to speak, though who knew what he was about to say, she stood on tiptoe and kissed him full on the mouth. And he was lost.

Chapter 12

Later, on the dusty sofa, still cradled in Colton's arms, Jewel listened to the steady thump of his heart and felt peace for the first time in years.

The feeling unnerved her.

Frowning, she twisted to peer up into his gaze. "Don't fall in love with me," she warned. She didn't know if she was talking to him or to herself.

He raised his head and gave her a lazy, sated smile. She felt it burn, low in her belly.

"No worries," he said. But the warmth in his dark eyes told her he was lying.

A small falsehood from one who claimed to

value truth, though she couldn't really blame him—cuddling with him like this made the temptation to lie to herself equally strong.

Especially now.

One thought kept nagging at her, one insidious, dangerous idea. *This thing between them could be beautiful, a once-in-a-lifetime pairing.*

Mates.

No. The word should be a curse word. She'd believed Leo was her mate, and look where that foolishness had gotten her. She needed to rein in the fantasy now.

Outside, birds sang. The breeze drifted in the open windows, making the cotton curtains billow and spin. This dusty little trailer was a far cry from the mansion she'd shared with Leo, yet she'd trade them instantly if given a choice. Right here, right now, being here with Colton, being held in his arms, made her feel cherished and loved.

Dangerous thoughts.

Still, she couldn't banish the contentment.

Time to be rational, practical. She'd made a bad choice before. This thing with Colton would be an even worse one.

She began to list the reasons. Though they were numerous, the two most important were all that should have mattered.

She was a shifter; he was not.

And one of the most notorious criminals in the United States wanted her dead. He'd get his wish soon, if she didn't figure out a way to change.

She refused to give in to self-pity.

Looking up, she found Colton watching her.

"You worry too much," he said.

Wanting to laugh and cry at the same time, she shook her head. "I'm serious, Colton."

"I am, too." Tracing the line of her jaw, he regarded her with eyes still dark from passion. "I'll tell you what. I won't fall for you, if you don't fall for me."

She went still. Even her heart stopped beating for half a second. How had he known? Chest tight, she tried to respond with an equally light-hearted comment, but couldn't get past the lump in her throat.

Finally, she managed to choke out a response. "You've got a deal."

"Good." He brushed a kiss near her ear, making her shiver.

If she turned the slightest bit, she could capture his mouth with hers....

No.

Scooting backward, she sat up. Swinging her legs over the side of the couch, she brushed her hair from her eyes. "There's a lot about me you don't know."

When he didn't respond, she couldn't help but look at him. He stretched, drawing her gaze to his flat, hard stomach and muscular chest. When he saw her looking, he gave her a lazy smile so full of masculine confidence her heart skipped.

"You think?" he teased. "I kind of doubt that."

"You hate secrets," she reminded him, a thread of desperation sneaking into her voice despite her effort to sound cool and collected. "And I have plenty of them."

His laughter made her smile.

"While I admire your tactic, it's not gonna work. I care about you, Jewel. Whether you like it or not."

Damn. If she responded in kind and told him the truth, she'd make things worse. Already the ties between them grew stronger, deeper.

Because she was afraid she might weep, she spun and headed back to the bathroom. No way would she let him see her cry.

That night, though Colton wanted her to sleep beside him in his double bed, Jewel deliberately chose the lumpy sofa. Best to put some distance between them. Especially since she planned to sneak out once he was asleep and attempt to release her wolf.

The urge had been building in her all day. Ever since she'd seen the wide open landscape, so perfect for a wild animal to run free, she'd known she had to try to change. This time, she had a feeling she'd either succeed or die trying.

But once she closed her eyes, to her complete surprise, she slept like a baby. No midnight run, no changing. She didn't wake at all until the sound of Colton rattling around the kitchen roused her.

Tentatively, she stretched, testing out her body. She felt…rested. For once, the wolf inside her was at peace.

Weird.

Sitting up and pushing back the blankets, she rubbed the back of her neck and yawned.

Colton looked up from the coffeemaker and grinned. "Morning."

"Good morning." Looking at him made her feel warm and dizzy. Hellhounds, she had it bad. "What's up?"

"I'm making coffee. I don't know about you, but I could sure use a cup."

"Me, too." She blushed. Was this how normal people acted after a night spent making love?

Having nothing to gauge by, Jewel murmured something more about how wonderful coffee sounded and padded toward the bathroom. She felt his gaze scorch her all the way there.

Damn, damn and double damn.

Once inside, she scrubbed her face so hard her skin turned red, then splashed cold water to rinse the soap off.

How had she let it come to this? Because she'd had no choice, she told herself, hating the way her hands shook, conscious of her ever-present need to change. Colton thought he knew her, but in fact he knew nothing about the real her. If he were to find out, he'd recoil in horror.

She'd heard the stories. Other shifters had tried to take human mates. Most failed. A few, a lucky few, succeeded. Jewel had never been even remotely lucky, not once in her life. She didn't expect she'd start now.

Colton watched as Jewel stalked to the bathroom. He wondered if she had any idea how beautiful she was. Though they'd made love twice the night before, he wanted her again. But he knew he'd have to be careful. She was skittish enough already.

When she emerged a few minutes later, he

handed her a mug of steaming coffee. "I put one cream and two sugars."

Accepting it, she shot him a surprised look. "How'd you know?"

"Watched you make it enough times, I guess."

While she sipped the coffee, his cell phone rang, making him jump. Flipping it open, he checked the caller ID. "Reba," he told Jewel. "It's about time she returned my call."

"Reba," she repeated. He could see her thoughts reflected in her expression. She'd believed the woman was her friend, but the Realtor obviously had another agenda.

He answered with a terse hello.

"Colton, I'm sorry. I meant to call back earlier, honestly I did. But there's been a lot going on." Reba sounded frantic. "I know I have a lot to explain and I promise I will, but not now. I know I was wrong, but…" She took a deep breath. "It's Bettina. She's missing and I think she's done something bad to Roy."

"Bettina?" Anger coiled in his stomach. "The woman who claimed to be my girlfriend? Who told Jewel I beat her up? And Roy, someone I thought was my friend, who lied about me, too? Why would I care where they are?"

"I understand. Really. But Colton, please listen.

This is serious. I think Bettina's crazy and she might have hurt Roy." Her voice caught. "He's in bad trouble."

Something in her voice gave him pause. Terror? "How so?"

"I love him, Colt. And he loves me. When he learned of Bettina's plans, he tried to stop her. I think she's taken him hostage."

One word stood out. "Plans? What plans?"

"She's working with Leo. He wants Jewel back and he wants to punish you for daring to touch her. I think he's paying Bettina an awful lot of money to help him."

Suddenly alert, now he listened. Bettina as Leo's operative? As they'd suspected, that meant her false accusations made a lot more sense. Getting Colton—Jewel's protector—out of the picture would make it easier to reach Jewel.

Reba coughed. "Colton, you've got to hide. Both you and Jewel. Get out of town before they find you."

Could Reba be trusted? He'd known her for five or six years. But she'd believed the worst of him, branding him abusive on the word of her lover and a stranger. He couldn't take the chance.

"We're gone. In a safe place. I'm going to keep Jewel safe."

"Good. Oh, and Floyd's been all over town looking for you. He knows you're with her, but isn't sure where. He's pretty angry. Something about you owing him a front-page story."

"I don't have time for that now. Thanks for the warning, though."

"Where *are* you?"

"You don't need to know. It's safer that way." Without another word, he closed the phone, ending the call.

When he relayed the conversation to Jewel, she stared. "He'll never find me here."

"Floyd's looking for me, too. He wanted me to write a story on you and I kept stalling him. But he's pissed." Now Colton paced. "I'm worried about him. If he thinks about it, he might figure out where we've gone. I brought him here last year during deer season."

A shadow crossed her face. "That's not good. I don't like that."

"Me either. But I don't know what else to do or where else we could go."

Fidgeting, she combed through her hair with her fingers. "I keep feeling like I should run as fast and as far away as I can. I feel…trapped."

"Don't." He took her arm. "Come on, let's go

for a walk. There are lots of trails here and pretty abundant wildlife this time of year."

She sighed. "Okay, but I need you to promise me something."

"Anything." He was only half joking.

"If Leo finds me, use my gun on him if you get the chance. But make sure it's loaded with silver bullets. Nothing else will work on him."

"Silver bullets again. What is he, a vampire?"

Finally, she smiled. "Wrong species. With vampires it's stakes through the heart and sunlight."

"That's right." He snapped his fingers. "Werewolves are the ones that only silver bullets can kill."

"Right. And fire. Silver bullets and fire."

"Are you saying Leo's a werewolf?" Still teasing, his grin faded as he realized she was not.

"I'm saying he's a monster." Jewel's voice trembled. "That's enough. Just remember what I told you. If you don't use the silver bullets, you won't get another chance. He'll kill you."

Though he waited, she didn't elaborate. He told himself he really didn't expect her to, after all. She wanted to keep her secrets close and he wouldn't pry. For now. With time, he wanted to know her inside and out.

"Come on." When he gave her arm a little tug, she came willingly. "I think you'll like what you see. It takes a special kind of person to appreciate this countryside."

"Special, huh? All right, show me."

He chose his favorite path, the one that meandered up toward the mesa. All went well until they startled a doe and a fawn. Bursting out of a clearing in front of them, the deer flashed past them on a mad run to safety.

"Oh!" Jewel wrenched from his grasp and, snarling, dropped to all fours. She began to convulse on the dirt path in front of him, growling low in her throat.

"Jewel!" he told her, going to his knees in front of her and trying to gather her close. "Hang in there. It's another seizure. You can make it through this."

Though no doubt it was due to the effects of the attack, she bared her teeth at him and snarled a warning.

Ignoring this, he stroked her hair as another violent spasm racked her slender body. "Come on, honey. You'll be okay. Relax, and it will pass."

"Pass?" She gasped, writhing and clawing at the air. "I'm trying to control this, really trying. Damn!"

"Control this?" His ex had used a similar expression when she'd been struggling against her addiction. "*Are* you using?"

"What?" She began to pant, short huffs of breath that reminded him of a woman in labor.

"Drugs. Are you using drugs?"

Doubled over, she groaned. "That again. Hell, no. For the last time, I am not on any type of drug. I only wish it were that simple."

He held her—and his tongue—as she continued to struggle. Gradually, the tremors subsided and her breathing became normal.

Supporting her back, he helped her sit up. "Are you all right?"

"All right?" A single tear rolled down her cheek. "I'm about as far from being all right as I can be." She buried her head in her hands, shaking. "God help me. I don't know what to do anymore." Her enlarged pupils and quickened breathing told him she battled the urgent desire that always plagued her after an episode.

"Let me help."

Firsts clenched, she didn't look up. "You can't." Her breathy voice belied her words and tugged at his own rising need.

"You'd be surprised."

It was a measure of her desperate attempt to maintain control that she didn't immediately take him up on his offer. Instead, her emerald gaze searched his face, as though trying to discern the hidden meaning of his words, while her chest rose and fell.

He wanted her to kiss him. Damn it, he craved her passion and her need and her body.

Forcing himself to hold still, he tried to wait. Surprisingly—or maybe not—he lost his battle for control before she did.

"Come here," he growled, slanting his mouth over hers and kissing her hard, the way he knew she needed. She met him halfway, growling low in her throat as she tore at his clothes.

Cloth tearing didn't matter. All that mattered was skin, his against hers, hers next to him. When he entered her, she was ready. She met him thrust for thrust, cry for cry.

When she clenched around him, he cried out her name. Their release came together, building until they shattered.

After, they held each other without speaking. One heartbeat, two, and he realized he wanted to hold her like that the rest of his life.

"Thank you," she said quietly, her face against his chest.

Flabbergasted, for a moment he didn't know what to say. Finally, he chuckled and kissed the top of her head. "No, thank *you*. Jewel, I want us to be together."

She went utterly still and, just as he had begun to curse his lack of eloquence, she shifted out of his embrace. She looked down at her hands, then back at his face. "You don't know what you're getting into."

"Hey." He brushed a wayward strand of red hair away from her cheek. "I'm a reporter. I've seen just about everything. I'll take that chance."

At the word *reporter,* her eyes widened. "You can't report on me, on this."

"Not if you don't want me to."

She moved away again, and he saw she trembled. Had he frightened her? Wanting to soothe, he stroked her arm.

"Stop," she said, a hitch in her voice.

He removed his hand. "What's wrong?"

"You're petting me like I'm an…animal."

"I'm sorry."

"No." Glancing at him, she gave him a tremulous smile, as though on the verge of tears. "Maybe you instinctively know the truth."

"What truth?"

She took a deep breath. "A relationship with me is not possible."

Fear. He understood fear intimately. "Don't worry. They'll catch Leo."

"It's not that."

Aching to touch her, instead he waited.

"When I have those…episodes, they're not seizures."

"No?"

"No. I was trying to change. Into a wolf. I'm a…shifter."

"Shifter? I'm not familiar with the term."

"Of course you're not." Her deep sigh sounded heartfelt. "Sometimes your folklore and legends refer to my kind as werewolves. That's what I am. Only something's wrong with me. I try to change into a wolf and can't. I think Leo did something to me." She searched his face for a reaction. "If I don't change soon, I'll die."

Colton swallowed. Whatever he'd expected, it wasn't this. Still, he could help her. Mental illness, though frightening, was still treatable. He found it odd that she'd shown no sign of this the entire time he'd known her.

"Are you sure?" he asked, as gently as he could.

Instead of answering, she lifted her chin, her glorious eyes flat and dead. "You think I'm crazy."

"No, I—"

"Being insane would be much simpler than what I'm dealing with. If I don't figure out what's wrong with me soon, and change, then I *will* be nuts." Scrabbling to her feet, she swayed slightly.

"I'm going about this all wrong. If you want to be with me, you have to know the truth. Worse, if you are going to have a prayer against Leo, you need to know about him."

"What are you saying?"

"Leo's a shifter, too. That's what makes him even more dangerous. That's why I have the silver bullets. Only those and fire can kill our kind."

He gathered her to him and held her, silently urging her to relax her stiff shoulders. "Jewel, what you've told me makes no sense."

"Why won't you believe me?" She pushed him away. "This is the most important thing I've ever said to you, and you won't listen."

"Can you blame me for doubting?"

"No, I can't." With a sigh, she reached out as if to touch him, pulling back at the last moment. "But we don't have much time. You said you wanted to help. You've got to decide whether to take what I say at face value or not. It's all about trust. Without trust, there can't be a relationship. Without trust, you might as well go."

Jamming his hands in his pockets, he could hear his own heart beating slow and steady while he stared at her. She waited, watching him, her gaze not wild-eyed and crazy, but steady and wary. What could he say? Suddenly he remembered when she'd been convulsing and he'd sworn he'd seen a wolf peering from the maelstrom of colors.

She believed what she was saying, thus she'd given him honesty to the best of her ability. He could do no less with her.

"Jewel, let me get you some professional help."

"No." She pushed past him, heading back toward the trailer. "I guess I have your answer."

For the space of three heartbeats he let her go. Then, he called after her. "Wait. Please."

She never broke stride.

"Prove it to me," he shouted, pushed to the limit. "Come on, you can't blame me for not believing in werewolves. I've never seen one. This is all outside my entire realm of experience."

This time she stopped. As she slowly turned, her choppy red hair blew in the breeze. "Prove it to you? How?"

"Change." Using her own word, he kept his expression serious. "Become a werewolf. Show me."

Again her hand went to her neck, to finger a necklace that wasn't there. "Hellhounds, if I could, I would. But like I just told you, I can't. I've been trying to change. That's what I was doing when you found me unconscious that first time. When you think I'm having a seizure, it's my body fighting to change. I can't."

"Was that what you were trying to do a minute ago?"

"Not on purpose. Actually, I was trying *not* to. When we saw that deer, my wolf-self…" Her words trailed off. "All right. I'll try once more. I don't know how else to prove it to you, except to try."

His pulse jumped, his stomach knotted. Ridiculous, unless he seriously thought she…no. At least delusions rarely physically hurt anyone. And maybe a demonstration would make her see she'd let her imagination take too deep of a hold. "Go ahead, try now. Maybe I can help you."

"Here?" She glanced around at the rocks and the dirt and the scrabbly, twisted trees bent sideways by the wind. "If I'm successful, stand back. Don't try to stop me or touch me."

He frowned. "Why not?"

"Because wolves don't like to be caged. I don't want to hurt you, even by accident. If I manage to change, I need to run free."

"I see." He studied her damaged beauty and wondered how best to help her. If he'd known she had mental-health issues, he could have gotten her help much sooner. But he hadn't known.

Watching him, she folded her arms. Waiting.

He nodded in encouragement, wondering if he was supposed to give her some sort of signal.

His nod must have been enough. Still watching him, she dropped to the ground, grimacing before she bowed her head.

Immediately, a hundred fireflies surrounded her.

He took another look. No, not fireflies, but sparkles of light, flashing and pulsating in a misty cloud of rainbow color.

The swirling, vibrant show obscured Jewel from his sight. Behind this, sounds—shuffling, snuffling, a groan.

"Are you all right?" he asked. "Is this another seizure?"

She didn't answer. Should he go to her? Try to push through the colors to reach her? What the hell was this? Had he lost his mind?

He rubbed his eyes. Still the sparkles, the random flecks of light, all colors of the rainbow. As if he were tripping on some bizarre drug.

"Jewel?" Finally he decided to push away his superstitious fear. He moved in, toward the spot where she'd been. "Are you in there? Answer me."

Instead of her voice, he heard a low growl.

A large dog. Maybe even a...wolf.

A *werewolf?*

No. No way. Not even possible.

But the hair on the back of his neck warned him. Danger! "Jewel?" Did she need his help?

No flashing lights were going to keep him from protecting her. He pushed forward, into the cloud of colors, hell-bent on reaching her.

There, on the ground on all fours, Jewel. But something... Blinking, he moved closer. As he watched, her beautiful face elongated; her nose became a snout. Fur sprouted all over her body, creamy skin becoming something else—the pelt of an animal. Of a beast.

A wolf.

He couldn't believe his eyes. Heart pounding, mouth dry, he croaked out her name. "Jewel?"

Even as her body contorted and changed, she raised her head to look at him. Tried to speak. Instead, she could only growl again.

The last remnants of swirling colors vanished.

So did Jewel. Protected by a screen of magic, her transformation from woman to animal had become complete. Instead of Jewel, a huge, ivory wolf stood where she'd knelt.

Watching him with her eyes. *Jewel.*

Colton reared back. Away. "What the hell?"

Like everyone else, he'd seen the movies, heard the stories, read the books. Werewolves didn't exist, except in the fertile imagination of writers and producers.

Did they?

Evidence to the contrary, the wolf snuffled, moving closer.

Telling himself not to run, Colton continued backing away. Though he didn't sense danger, he couldn't fathom what had happened. Jewel had...what? Changed into a wolf? Part of him screamed *no way* and wanted to look for the smoke and mirrors, the hidden cameras.

Though she'd claimed she could, she couldn't really have become a wolf. This was reality, not some alternate world in a paranormal novel or pulp horror movie.

Still, he took a step back.

The wolf lowered its head, still watching him. Jewel's beautiful emerald eyes looked exotic in the lupine face.

No. Not. Possible.

Yet it was.

She'd called herself a shifter. She'd tried to tell him the truth.

Jewel, beautiful, sensuous Jewel, was a werewolf.

A werewolf? He shook his head, trying to make sense of the illogical.

There was no such thing. Was there?

The beast moved closer, still intently focused on him.

Colton stumbled. Cursing, he righted himself,

hoping the wolf wouldn't attack. Even though he could barely wrap his mind around it, facts were facts. As a seasoned reporter, he could force himself to recognize them, even when the shock of the impossible threatened to make his stomach heave.

A werewolf. He'd made love—several times—to a werewolf.

No escaping the truth. She hadn't been lying. Jewel, his Jewel, the woman he'd been entertaining thoughts of making a permanent part of his life—wasn't even human.

Reeling, Colton staggered away, unable to look at the ivory-coated wolf. Either he'd gone crazy or the world had become his own personal twilight zone.

He knew better than to run, though every instinct screamed it. Instead, he took off at a brisk walk, heading for the untamed hills where other wild animals roamed.

Maybe if he walked enough, far enough, long enough, hard enough, reality would return.

Instead, new reality refused to leave him. At first the wolf kept pace with him, skirting the trees as Colton climbed the old hunting path toward the bluff.

Finally, when he would not acknowledge its presence, the animal veered off, heading toward

the wooded area and, most likely, fresh game.
Wild pigs and deer inhabited these woods. A feast
for an experienced hunter—or a hungry wolf.

An image flashed in his mind. He saw the ivory
wolf bringing down a doe, ripping out its throat,
blood dripping from sharp, white teeth.

Jewel's teeth.

No! He groaned. How could he reconcile the
woman he'd begun to care for with *this?*

Chapter 13

He wandered the hills for hours, unable to face the mess his world had just become. Finally, as the sun began to descend toward the horizon, he headed back for the cabin, weary in body and weary in soul. By now Jewel should had changed back to her human self, so he could talk to her.

Hopefully, she hadn't gone. Though part of him wished she had. Confused, shocked and honestly afraid, he didn't know what he wanted. What he felt. He was no longer certain of anything.

The thought made him wince.

She'd told him she had secrets. In a hundred,

million years, he'd never imagined they'd be anything like this.

Yet picturing a future without her was so bleak, he ached when he thought of it.

He'd done a lot of soul searching and agonizing while walking the land. As a reporter, he was trained to work with facts. Ignorance bred fear. He needed to talk with Jewel, learn more about her species, and try to banish his instinctual terror.

If he wanted them to have a chance, he had no choice.

Climbing the path to the mobile home, the first thing he noticed was the blood. The path was tainted by it; huge splatters discolored the grass, the leaves, the dirt. Had Jewel, in her wolf form, killed a deer or pig and brought the carcass here to feast?

He rather doubted that.

Heart pounding, he ran for the front door. Crimson stained everything, the ground, the porch and the front door. The knot in his gut twisted.

"Jewel?" he called, hoping against hope she was here, that she'd answer. On the porch, he slipped, his sneakers sliding in the fresh blood— he turned and raised his voice, calling out over the vast expanse of land. "Jewel?"

No answer.

Bracing himself, he entered the house.

Inside, he found Roy, bound and semiconscious, a baseball bat on the floor beside him. Reba's warning about Bettina ringing in his ears, Colton crouched beside the man he'd once thought of as his friend.

Damn.

Quickly, gently, he removed the ropes and untied the gag, easing it from Roy's mouth.

"Water," Roy croaked, blinking at him.

He got a glass, helping Roy hold it to his mouth as he greedily gulped. When he paused to take a breath, Colton set the glass on the floor.

"Roy, what happened? Where's Jewel?"

Wincing, Roy gave a long, shuddering sigh. "Bettina has her. She's taking her to Leo."

A coldness spread through Colton's chest. "Bettina? How?"

"She knocked Jewel out with a tranquilizer dart." Sitting up, Roy rubbed his head and groaned. "Floyd figured out where you'd gone and broadcast it around town. I think Bettina hurt him. Right before she held a gun on me and made me get in the car with her." His gaze flickered away and he licked his lips, as he'd always done when he got inventive with the truth.

There'd be time later to ask Roy why he'd lied. Colton knew the lengths men would go to for love.

"Where?" Colton asked. "Tell me where they've gone."

Roy took a deep breath, his bright blue eyes glittering strangely. "I don't know."

Colton closed his eyes. Jewel's worst nightmare.

When he started for the door, Roy followed.

"What are you going to do?"

Turning, Colton looked at the man he'd only thought he'd known, his expression grim. "I'm going to find them, of course. I promised Jewel I'd protect her."

"I can't let you do that," Roy said. Then he hit Colton with the baseball bat.

Finally—changed! As a wolf for the first time in months, Jewel yearned to tear off over the rocky terrain, thrilling to the feel of the hard-packed earth under her sensitive paws. Spirit soaring, she stretched her muscles. Her wolf body felt strong, right, though too long unused.

But the man was too important to her. She'd seen the shock and terror on his handsome face. Even as wolf, she'd felt a pang.

He had to understand. This was too important.

She crept closer, keeping her body low to the ground, in the subservient position so he'd know she wasn't a threat.

Instead, he stumbled backward, one hand out as if to ward her off.

She paused. Cocked her head. Inhaled. The sharp tang of perspiration colored with fear filled her sensitive nose.

Fear? Colton was afraid of *her?*

She whimpered, trying to communicate. No matter the body, she was the same soul. But he didn't understand and took off, away from her, away from the mobile home. Out into the rolling hills, exactly where she wanted to be.

First, she kept pace with him, willing him to touch her, to call her to him. But after awhile, the sensations were too much for her. The myriad scents and textures of this new wilderness called to her animal nature. Too long denied, she finally veered away from Colton, heading out on her own.

The dry grass felt prickly under her paws, and in the hot wind she caught a whiff of smoke. Somewhere, a fire burned. But not here.

The sun beat down, warming her fur, making her lift her muzzle to the sky and bare her teeth. Chancing across deer spoor, she sniffed, following the herd's trail up the rocky mesa, were she could see for miles.

Forgetting Colton, forgetting everything of the

human world for a few joyful hours, she reveled and played, ran and rolled.

Grass, sky and sun. What more could one ask for?

She was wolf. Finally at home in her body again. Free.

With no way to keep track of time, after an hour or maybe six had passed, she felt pleasantly tired. Her stomach rumbled with hunger.

Now, she would hunt. She scented and trailed a wild pig, bringing down the small boar and ripping his throat out before eating her fill. She forgot to be on the watch for danger. Sated, happy, she grew careless.

Cardinal rule of shifters—always remain alert for danger. If one eye closed, keep the other eye open.

She nearly stumbled upon Bettina, crouched and hiding in a small grove of leafy trees. The wind blew in the wrong direction, carrying Bettina's scent away from her. If the woman hadn't made a sudden move, Jewel would have walked into a trap.

Disbelieving that she'd actually seen the woman before she'd scented her, Jewel backed quietly away to hide in tall grass and watch. The wind shifted and now she caught Bettina's scent, wrinkling her snout at the mingled odors of perfume and perspiration. As a wolf, her sense of smell was forty times that of a human.

She crouched low to the ground and hid under a group of bushes, watching. Bettina! The woman who'd claimed Colton had beaten her to within an inch of her life.

The woman was up to no good. As a matter of fact, even as a wolf, Jewel realized Bettina's presence could only mean one thing.

Somehow, Leo had found her.

As wolf, Jewel wanted to take Bettina down. She readied herself for the leap, tensing her strong leg muscles, glad of her lithe, sleek strength.

But, at the last minute, she hesitated. The human side of her, in charge for so long, held her wolf-self back.

She stumbled. Leaves rustled.

At the sound, Bettina spun. Too late, Jewel saw the tranquilizer gun in the woman's hand. She knew an instant's sharp pinprick of pain as the dart struck, then nothing.

Colton saw the bat coming and dodged, just enough for the blow to glance off his shoulder rather than his head. He staggered back, thinking fast. "What the hell, Roy? Why are you doing this?"

"Because of what you did to Bettina, you bastard." Roy came at him again.

Colton dodged. "I don't even know her."

"So you say," Roy spat. "But she told me. She knew you before, when you were still married. She told me all about what you did. She wasn't lying. She loved you, Colton. And I love her. I dated Reba as a ploy to get her to help us. And Bettina knows Leo." He swung the bat again.

Colton leaped up, snatching it out of midair. Swing interrupted, Roy stumbled as Colton jerked him toward himself.

The bat went flying, slamming into the wall and knocking down the clock, which shattered.

Colton grabbed Roy, twisting him and holding his arms. "You're crazy, Roy. Think. You've known me for years. You know better."

"How many times do I have to say it? I saw what you did to Bettina," Roy snarled. "You're going to pay."

"I don't have time for this." Colton shook the man. "Where's Jewel?"

"If I say I don't know," Roy taunted, "are you going to beat it out of me?"

"Don't tempt me. I'll ask one more time. Where's Jewel?"

"Bettina said she was taking her to Dallas. To Leo."

"Why? Why would you help a criminal like him?"

"To punish you," Roy bit out. "You always thought you were superior, even back at Channel Four. Everyone loved you, until you turned your back on them and left town." He snorted. "You even refused to come back, even though you had a job most men would kill for handed to you on a silver platter. What makes you think you're so much better than me?"

Colton didn't even bother to try and dignify that comment. "Jewel doesn't deserve this. Leo will kill her."

Roy frowned. "What her own husband does with her is not my problem."

"*Ex*-husband." Colton ground out the words.

"Whatever. All I know is, Leo promised to pay. Bettina delivers her, Leo hands over the money. And we escape to Trinidad."

"Bettina left you here. Do you really think she'll come back?"

"She doesn't have to." Roy laughed. "I'm supposed to go there, too. With you. Leo plans to make you pay for touching his woman."

"Jewel is not his woman." Colton let Roy go, shoving him away hard. Snatching up the baseball bat, Colton brandished it over one shoulder as he backed toward the door.

"Where are you going?" Roy asked, sneering.

"After them. I've got to save Jewel."

"Oh, yeah? How are you gonna find them?"

"Good point." Colton grabbed the rope that had bound Roy earlier. "Hands behind your back. You're coming with me and you're going to show me the way."

"Works for me." Roy grinned without a trace of fear. "All they said was to bring you. They didn't say how."

Colton drove like a madman. An hour later, they'd reached Fort Worth. Speeding through the mid-cities was tricky. He knew from experience that there were a lot of speed traps. Sill, he kept the accelerator to the floor.

His luck held. No one stopped him.

When he finally exited 183 and drove to an industrial area of Dallas, he made the final turn and realized Roy had directed him to an abandoned warehouse.

Parking, he glanced around. The area appeared deserted, though he knew that wasn't true.

Most of the windows were either boarded up or protected with black, wrought-iron burglar bars. The sidewalks were deserted; not even a stray vagrant cluttered the doorways.

A bad part of town. But perfect for whatever Leo had in mind.

Colton looked around for observers or cameras. He saw nothing. Good. He glanced at his passenger, still tied. Roy stared back, smirking.

Reaching into the glove box, Colton pulled out Jewel's pistol, glad he had the weapon. Remembering what she'd said, he loaded the silver bullets, slipping the metal box in his back pocket in case he needed more ammo. Then, turning to Roy, he slammed him on the back of the head with the butt of the gun, knocking him unconscious. Colton got out of the Jeep.

A movement made him tense. The warehouse door slowly opened. Heart pounding, he watched, waiting.

But the door only swung in the breeze. No one appeared behind it, though whoever had opened it could have moved back into the shadows.

Taking a deep breath, Colton prayed for strength. Then he headed for the door.

Whatever drugs the dart gun had carried hit Jewel hard, though not hard enough to keep her from changing back to human. Several times, she struggled to swim up to the edge of consciousness. Each time she slid back down into the black hole of oblivion before she could break the surface of the water. It didn't surprise her, this subconscious use of water analogies. The lake—and Colton—had become the center of her existence, a shining symbol of hope.

She refused to let that spark go out.

Stubborn, she kept trying. She wanted to open her eyes. But the lids felt too heavy. Finally, after her fifth or fiftieth attempt, she succeeded. They'd put her in a small, windowless room. Most likely a storage closet. There were no clocks, no pictures, nothing but unfinished walls and the cold cement floor. She had no idea how much time had passed—hours or days—but she was still alive.

Leo would keep her that way, until he'd had his fun. Knowing him, the sadistic bastard would torture her for months, maybe years, until she finally expired or he accidentally killed her.

But she was still optimistic. She had one advantage. Unless Bettina'd had time to tell, Leo didn't know she could change again. If she could speed up the process of becoming a wolf, she could rip out his throat before he had time to change himself. Not entirely impossible, and right now, her only chance.

Clank. The sound of a lock turning, a bolt sliding back. Unable to help herself, she tensed, then feigned unconsciousness. Eyes screwed shut, she worked to slow her breathing, to steady the fine trembling of her hands.

The door opened with a creak. Someone entered the room.

Despite herself, her nostrils flared. Leo's scent. Pungent. Strong. Evil. She swallowed hard.

He didn't speak and she kept her eyes closed. She heard the sound of metal rasping against metal. Her heart started pounding, feeling as though it would leap from her chest. Had he brought a knife? Knowing he could cut her until her skin shredded like ribbon and she wouldn't die?

Giving up the pretense, she raised her head and saw he waited, silently watching her. Silver glinted in his hands. Not a knife, but some kind of pendant. Prison hadn't changed him as far as she could tell; if anything the experience had taught him to hone his cruelty to an even sharper edge. His dark gaze glinted with malice.

"Finally, the princess awakes."

Princess had been his nickname for her, given only when he meant to do something painful to her to give himself pleasure. Unable to help herself, she shuddered. His voice repulsed her. She knew if she could succeed in keeping her face expressionless, not allowing him to see her instinctive terror, he wouldn't be pleased. Good. He was going to hurt her no matter what. She'd deny him his satisfaction as long as she could.

She gave him her best blank stare. "Why don't you kill me now and be done with this, Leo."

Though she'd expected it, his laugh chilled her to the marrow of her bones. "Now that would deprive me of my fun, wouldn't it? You know better than anyone I've always found my greatest pleasure in torture."

At least he didn't try to claim she'd enjoyed his vile acts, too.

"What, nothing to say?" he taunted. "Cat got your tongue?"

Though she wanted to speak, to pop off some snappy and snide comment, the old terror clogged her throat. Too many years of conditioning and pain, too many times of being shown exactly who was boss in their marriage, and why.

Heart pounding, she had to look away. Looking at him sickened her.

As if he knew, he came closer. She tried to lift her hands and dimly realized she was tied. "How did you find me?"

His grin was pure evil. "Your necklace. That stupid, ugly piece of jewelry you never took off. When you sent it off for repair that time, I had a tracking device installed in the wolf charm. That way, I always knew where you were."

She closed her eyes. He'd even defiled the one

thing she'd thought solely hers. Opening them again, she chanced a quick glance at him before staring at the wall to his right. "From prison?"

"I had help." Glee rang in his voice. "Though keeping you from changing was all me."

Since she knew he'd tell her whether she wanted to know or not, she kept silent.

"Contacts been bothering you lately?"

"What?" She couldn't believe he'd managed to do something to her contacts. *"How?"*

"The solution." Grin full of pride, he tilted his head. "You always bought two large bottles of cleaning solution, so you'd have a backup. I doctored those."

So every time she'd cleaned her contacts, she'd dosed herself again. When she'd lost the bottle in the fire and had purchased a new untainted bottle, she'd finally been able and change. In the meantime, Leo's interference had nearly killed her. Hellhounds, how she hated this man.

"Now it's your turn to talk." His voice turned serious. "I've heard you took another lover."

From past experience, she knew if she argued, or even spoke, his punishment would be even more harsh.

When she didn't respond, he moved closer still. Close enough that his breath tickled her cheek, close enough for him to change and rip out her throat, if he wanted.

"He's on his way here. I'll let you watch me kill him for daring to touch you. You're mine. You'll always be mine."

Pain knifed through her. Despite that, she lifted her chin and met his gaze, her own unflinching. The depths of the fury simmering in his eyes told her he meant his words.

Of course he did. Leo Licciardoni always killed when he said he would. He believed that alone made him a man of his word, despite his many other lies.

He turned to go, pausing to let his gaze roam over her in such an intimate way he made her shudder.

"By the way," he said, his tone indifferent. "I got rid of your parents, too. Their car crash? Me. The ensuing fire? Yep, you guessed it. Once they were gone, you had nowhere left to turn, now did you?"

Flabbergasted, her shock turned to rage. "If you'd told me that when we were married, I would have found a way to kill you, even if I had to kill myself to do it."

The bastard laughed. "I should have told you. It would have been fun to let you try." Shoving a gag in her mouth, he tied it tightly and left, closing the door behind him.

Though tears prickled at her eyes, she refused to cry. No way would she give Leo the satisfaction. He'd killed her parents. How she despised him. And now Colton's life was in danger because of her. She had to figure out a way to save him.

Chapter 14

Taking a deep breath, Colton entered the building. Damp and gloomy, the smell of musk and perspiration brought to mind death and decay.

Where was Jewel? Was she being held here?

He moved forward. His footsteps echoed on concrete, making the dust swirl. Looking down, he could see other footprints had disturbed the dusty layers. Mixed among the human marks, he saw animal tracks, like those of a large dog or a...wolf.

Jewel? Or worse, had Leo become his wolf alter ego?

Colton continued on. Now he had the advantage. Unless Leo's men had seen him enter, they weren't expecting him yet. They were waiting for Roy to bring him, bound and unconscious.

His plan was simple. Find Jewel, get out, call the police.

He'd accomplished the first objective rather easily. So easily, he felt the wrongness in the air like an electrical charge on his skin. He moved across the large room toward the office area and looked in the first small office. There he found Jewel, gagged and tied to a chair.

Not questioning blind luck, he freed her and helped her to her feet.

"Come with me."

Instead of moving, she stared at him hard. "No. This is a trap! You're not safe." Yanking her hand from his, she gave him a shove. "Go."

"And leave you? No way." He grabbed her arm and pulled her toward the door. "Let's go."

Though she gave him an exasperated look, she went with him, rushing toward the door and freedom.

Halfway across the main room, they heard a click. A supernova of light flashed, blinding them. Someone had turned on an immense spotlight, trained only on Colton.

Pinned in the illumination, a highlighted target,

they froze. Caught in a spider's web. If the bad guys were going to shoot them, Colton couldn't see to fight back.

Despite that, the gun felt heavy in his pocket, its weight reassuring. Maybe having it loaded with silver bullets was only foolishness, but after what he'd seen Jewel do, he couldn't help but believe.

Legend said silver bullets killed werewolves.

Either way, being armed was better than nothing.

"Move forward." A voice came from beyond the light.

"Not Leo," Jewel whispered. One of his henchmen or bodyguards, no doubt. Colton wanted the actual man.

With nowhere else to go, they did as they were told.

The spotlight clicked off. Still temporarily blinded, Colton squinted, trying to find his adversary.

Finally, he could make out two men standing by a black metal industrial staircase. They flanked a huge wolf with fur so black, it blended with the shadows. Leo?

Colton took a step forward. Jewel's touch on his arm stopped him.

"That's him." Despair and anger warred in her voice.

The wolf moved also, closing half the distance,

still flanked by the bodyguards. Colton refused to show fear, though his gut tightened.

When only a few feet separated them, the animal stopped. Colton did, too. He moved his hand to rest on the butt of the gun, trying to get ready before the wolf attacked.

The wolf snarled. But it didn't move, staring up at him with an intelligence that was frighteningly human. Colton knew then that he'd have to make the first move.

"Don't," Jewel urged, low-voiced.

Ignoring the warning, Colton didn't even hesitate. Yanking the gun free, he flicked off the safety and drew a bead on the wolf.

Immediately, the two bodyguards leaped in front of Leo, protecting him. Colton found himself baring his own teeth, as if he were the animal.

"Move back," one man growled.

Not wanting to endanger Jewel's and his chances, Colton did as he was told, moving slowly backward until he had the wall behind him.

Jewel did the same. Her fury and fear radiated off her in waves so strong even Colton could pick up on them. Despite that, when she met his gaze, he saw not despair, nor blind rage, but fierce resolve. He hoped his own expression mirrored hers. After all, he had the gun, still pointed at them. And loaded with silver bullets.

Still, he would only be able to take out one before he was overcome and the animal's razor sharp teeth tore into him.

As if sensing his thoughts, the wolf poked his massive head around one bodyguard's legs, baring his teeth and growling low in his throat.

Despite himself, Colton shifted his weight uneasily. At any moment they could rush him. "I promise I'll take out as many of you as I can before I die," he threatened.

The guards merely laughed.

"Jewel," Colton spoke her name without taking his eyes off their enemy. "Head for the door. Now."

The wolf snarled, louder and more threatening. A promise. Despite that, Jewel inched along the wall as Colton had asked.

"I wouldn't do that if I were you." Roy's voice. Colton cut his gaze toward the exit. Roy had regained consciousness and somehow managed to free himself. The furious look he gave Colton promised retribution.

Roy was the least of his problems. Concentrating again on the bodyguards and the beast, Colton kept the pistol leveled. "Move, and I shoot."

As though given an order, Roy grabbed Jewel.

She shoved him and he backhanded her. Hard. Her head snapped back, against the cement wall. She cried out and slumped to the ground.

With the gun still pointed at the guards—and Leo—Colton moved forward. But before he could reach her, the wolf went for Roy, moving so fast it was a blur. It attacked, leaping high. Roy screamed, his cry turning into a dying gurgle as the animal savagely ripped out his throat. Blood gushed from his destroyed neck.

Expressions horrified, the other two body-guards backed away. One of them swore under his breath.

The wolf raised his bloody muzzle and snarled again.

Now. Colton had a clear shot. He swung around to bring the weapon to bear on Leo, aimed, and one of the bodyguards knocked it from his hand. The gun went skittering across the cement floor. Both Colton and the other man went for it.

The other man reached it first. Dropping to his knees and pivoting in a movement that screamed *military,* he pointed the gun at Colton.

"Enough," Jewel shouted. Again the sparks flared, flashed, a multihued burst of light in fast motion. When the brightness faded, an ivory-coated wolf stood in her place. She moved toward the other wolf, snarling.

The black wolf raised his bloody muzzle and growled a warning.

Wolf-Jewel responded in kind.

Behind Roy's bloody corpse, someone screamed. Another woman ran into the room, skidding to a stop at the edge of the shadows and dropping to her knees over the body.

"Nooooo," she cried. "Not Roy." When she raised her head, Colton recognized her. Betty Keyes, his ex-wife's best friend.

Bettina. Another piece of the puzzle fell into place. She'd hated him for sending Paula to prison. When she'd hooked up with Roy, she'd seduced him into exacting vengeance. How fortunate for Leo that he'd come across the two of them.

A low growl brought Colton's attention back to the wolves.

Black wolf and white, Leo and Jewel faced off, circling each other. Jewel showed her teeth, snarling again. The sound reverberated as Leo responded in kind.

They sprang for each other.

Colton saw a flash of metal as Bettina lifted a gun. Instead of aiming at him, she pointed her weapon at the wolves.

He cursed, eyeing his own gun, now aimed at him. His captor laughed. "Move and I'll shoot you."

Colton guessed Bettina meant to try and kill both wolves, avenging Roy's death and getting revenge on Colton by killing Jewel.

He'd die before he let that happen.

The wolves broke apart, bleeding. They resumed their circling, intent on each other.

"Bettina, put the gun away," the other bodyguard said. "You can't kill them. They can't even kill each other."

His admonishment didn't appear to faze Bettina. Mouth pulled back in a grimace eerily similar to the wolves, she leveled her pistol on the white wolf.

Colton was betting she had silver bullets.

As she sighted her gun, again the wolves sprang at each other, teeth snapping.

Bettina frowned. Her steady hold on her weapon wavered.

The other guard moved stealthily along the back wall, heading for Bettina. When he rounded the back wall, his foot connected with something, making a sound.

Bettina spun and shot him. He didn't even have time to scream. Shot through the heart, he died instantly.

Colton wondered if she'd kill him next.

But paying Colton no heed, once again she tried to draw a bead on the ivory wolf, waiting for them to break away. Still locked on each other, black fur melded with white. And blood. So much blood.

Finally, they sprang apart. Spent, sides heaving, they stood separated by a few feet, each gathering strength for another attack.

Bettina grinned. She raised her gun. Squeezed the trigger and fired.

Colton's guard shot her.

Screeching, she jerked and fell. While the guard's attention was on her, Colton body-slammed him. The man went down, his head cracking on concrete, very still.

Colton grabbed his gun and pivoted, hoping he wasn't too late.

But just as Colton was sighting, the black wolf staggered and reeled backward. Leo crashed to the ground, limbs splayed, and lay unmoving in a pool of rapidly spreading crimson.

Bettina's shot had found a mark.

Panting, the white wolf swayed, but stayed on her feet, sides heaving, eyeing the fallen wolf.

Colton went to him, checking for a pulse.

"He's dead. Bettina must have had silver bullets."

"I did," Bettina grunted, trying to sit up. "I wanted to kill her, too, and then you. Roy wasn't supposed to die." Moving jerkily, she tried to rise. She crouched halfway up, bleeding profusely, pushing herself up on her knees, clawing at air. Before Colton knew what she meant to do, she dove for the guard she'd killed, sliding on blood-slicked cement. She went for his weapon, coming up triumphantly with it in her hand. Squinting, she brought up her gun and tried to aim at Colton, knowing regular bullets wouldn't kill Jewel.

Colton charged her. Reaching her before she could take aim, he knocked the weapon out of her hand. She tried to hit him, but collapsed instead, twitching and moaning in pain.

He turned. Behind him, Jewel made a sound. Again the swirl of lights surrounded her as she quickly changed back from wolf to human. Panting, she grabbed up her bloodstained clothes and dressed, watching him warily.

"Are you hurt?" he asked.

She shrugged. "A little. Shifters heal fast. I'll be all right."

"She didn't shoot you?"

"No." They both looked at Bettina, who'd passed out. "You'd better call for an ambulance."

He reached in his pocket for his cell phone and dialed 911.

When he looked up again, Jewel was gone.

Heart heavy, he went through the motions. The police and emergency personnel arrived within minutes and then there were statements to give, questions to answer. After dealing with the police and the interrogation, Colton also was exhausted. Still, he called the newspaper to make sure Floyd was all right. The man's cranky disposition improved when Colton promised him the scoop on the story of the year.

Still unconscious, Bettina was loaded into the ambulance and rushed off to Parkland Hospital, and the two guards' bodies were taken to the morgue. Though Colton had relinquished his gun to the police for ballistics tests, it was obvious from the bullets that Bettina had killed both men.

Finally, the crime-scene unit finished their investigation, though they'd been puzzled about the dead wolf. Colton had claimed it had been a vicious guard dog, which had torn out Roy's throat. He told them the dogs had run away.

Once all that was over, the police left him alone.

Wrung dry and exhausted, Colton wondered about Jewel. Aching, he tried to figure out where she might have gone. What hurt the most was knowing she hadn't even given them a chance. How could he fight for her if she ran away?

He had no idea where to even begin looking. With Leo dead, perhaps she'd go home, back to New York and that town where she'd grown up.

Because Colton couldn't guess, he decided he'd head home to the lake and try to sort things out.

When he reached the Jeep, his heart stopped.

There. Jewel. Asleep in the back. A little bed-raggled with her tattered and bloodstained dress, but unhurt and breathing. All woman.

Joy flooded him, so fierce and deep he couldn't breathe. He felt as if he'd been granted a miracle, as if a hopelessly impossible dream had been allowed to finally come true.

Moving carefully so he wouldn't wake her, he climbed in the front seat and started the engine.

She raised her head and looked at him, fatigue making circles under her sleepy eyes. "Colton?"

"Go back to sleep," he told her, smiling.

"Where are we going?"

He smiled tenderly. "Home. I'm taking you home."

"No." Pushing herself up to a sitting position, she frowned. "We need to talk."

"Later." He gave a meaningful glance back toward the warehouse. One police cruiser still remained, the officers inside finishing up. "It's a forty-five-minute drive back to the lake. Let's go there and get some rest first."

Though she still looked uncertain, she finally nodded. Climbing into the front seat, she fastened her seat belt and stared straight ahead. Ten minutes into the drive, she fell back asleep, snuggling into the seat. Eventually, her head came to rest on his shoulder, and he was content.

Rarely done, changing twice in one day had wiped Jewel out. Though she wanted to stay awake—needed to stay awake and settle things with Colton—the multiple changes and the fight had taken their toll. When sleep claimed her for the second time, she hoped she wouldn't dream.

Too often in her life she had dared to dream, only to have her hopes crushed.

"Jewel, we're here." His voice, Colton's. The man she'd come to love despite all the odds against them. Struggling, she tried to open her eyes, failing completely.

She felt him release her seat belt. When he lifted her in his arms and set her feet on the ground, she fought to gain energy to keep from crumpling in a boneless heap on the grass.

Wobbly legged, she succeeded.

He cradled her against his chest, supporting her, letting her lean on him as they made their way into his house. She listened to his heartbeat, strong and steady under her cheek, and tried to imagine life without him.

A wolf without a mate. She supposed that was only fitting. She'd already lost her Pack. An outsider probably should get used to being alone.

Only thing was—she didn't want to.

She wanted Colton. She wanted it all.

Colton helped her to the couch, worrying that her injuries were more severe than they appeared. She didn't wake again, and he covered her with a blanket and let her sleep, taking the chair near her side.

The calls started coming in the next morning. ABC, NBC, CBS, FOX, and CNN—all the networks left messages on his machine. They all wanted exclusives with Jewel, thanks to Floyd and his big mouth.

Colton ignored them, waiting for her to awaken.

Hearing the ping of the coffeepot finishing brewing, he went and got himself a cup. When he returned, she sat up, her hair tousled, her expression guarded.

"Mornin'," he said. "Would you like some coffee?"

She gave a hesitant nod.

Absurdly tongue-tied, he brought it, burning his mouth by drinking his own too fast. She sipped hers, peering at him over the rim of her cup. "Are you ready to talk?"

He nodded, trying to push past the emotion clogging his throat and find the right words.

Absolutely still, she watched him. Her haunted eyes shone brilliant green from her pale face.

"I..." Still struggling, he didn't know where to begin. Or how. He who was so good with words on paper couldn't seem to string together a coherent sentence to save his life.

A minute ticked by, then another. When Colton still didn't speak, she dipped her chin once in acknowledgment. Hurt had made her gaze dark. "I'd better go."

He knew if she left this time, she wouldn't be back.

God help him, he couldn't let her. She'd stayed, given them a chance, and he didn't know what to say.

Except this. "I love you."

She froze, her shoulders rigid, keeping her back to him. He kept talking, hoping she'd turn to face him.

"I love you, Jewel. Both parts of you. I know

you've heard that before, from someone you thought you could trust, but this is me."

Her strangled sound could have been one of pain, or of joy.

"Me, Jewel. You know me better than I know myself. I thought…" His voice broke, and for a moment he couldn't go on. "I thought my life was over, hell—I *wanted* my life to be over when my daughter died." Speaking of it, he felt the old familiar pain lessen somewhat.

"When I learned her own mother, my own wife, had killed her, I was furious at myself for not seeing it coming, for not stopping it. Sixteen years old! She'd barely begun to live. But I'd been too tied up in my own life, in my career, and I missed the signs."

Slowly she turned, her gaze soft and full of compassion. "You blame yourself?"

Rage filled him, clogging his throat so he couldn't speak. Rage and self-loathing, but as he looked at her, both melted away. "I did, once."

"It wasn't your fault, Colton."

Though he jerked his head in a nod, he continued on as if he hadn't heard her words. "I would have traded my life for hers in a heartbeat, but I couldn't. Do you realize how much I would trade to have my little girl back?"

Nodding, Jewel sniffed. Wondering, he realized she was crying. Silent tears made silver tracks down her too-pale skin.

"Why are you telling me this now?" she asked.

"Because I've learned what's important in this life. Damned if I'm letting you go. I'd regret it the rest of my life."

She stared, her expression guarded. He rushed to continue, the words now pouring from him like a flood. "You're important to me. We have a chance, you and I. Do you realize how special this thing between us can be? How rare?"

She moved forward hesitantly, like a sleep-walker still deep in the throes of a dream. "You saw me change." She wiped away her tears with the back of her hand. "You can't pretend you never saw that, or that it never happened. It's who I am, what I am. Part of me."

Cupping her face in his hands, he kissed the tip of her nose. "I know what I saw and I realize what you are. I want to love both parts of you. I want to learn more about your kind, your people. But first, I want you to try."

Mouth working, she appeared to be trying not to cry. "Try what?"

"Try to love me the way I love you."

"I don't have to try. I already do. But—"

He hushed her with a kiss, this time on the mouth and deep and long and full of his heart. When he came up for air, she grinned, a big, wolfish, utterly feminine grin.

"Convince me again," she said.

Laughing, he did.

* * * * *

Don't miss the next mystical and romantic story
in Karen Whiddon's **THE PACK** *miniseries*
Coming to bookstores in March 2007.
Only from Silhouette Nocturne.

This February…

Catch NASCAR Superstar **Carl Edwards** in
SPEED DATING!

Kendall assesses risk for a living—
so she's the last person you'd
expect to see on the arm of a
race-car driver who thrives on the
unpredictable. But when a bizarre
turn of events—and NASCAR
hotshot Dylan Hargreave—inspire
her to trade in her ever-so-structured
existence for "life in the fast lane"
she starts to feel she might be
on to something!

Collect all 4 debut novels in the Harlequin NASCAR series.

SPEED DATING
by *USA TODAY* bestselling author
Nancy Warren

THUNDERSTRUCK
by Roxanne St. Claire

HEARTS UNDER CAUTION
by Gina Wilkins

DANGER ZONE
by Debra Webb

On sale February 2007

---

www.eHarlequin.com   NASCARFEB

HARLEQUIN® *Romance*®

What a month!

In February watch for

Rancher and Protector

Part of the Western Weddings miniseries

BY JUDY CHRISTENBERRY

The Boss's Pregnancy Proposal

BY RAYE MORGAN

Also in February, expect
MORE of what you love
as the Harlequin Romance line
increases to six titles per month.

nocturne™

**Don't miss the next book in
the *Guardians* miniseries!**

NEVERMORE

MAUREEN CHILD

Reborn after Queen Isabella ordered her lover's
death, Santos accepted eternal life in exchange
for protecting humanity. For centuries, he's kept
himself secluded in a hillside mansion until he
meets his Destined Mate. With the threat of her
imminent extinction ticking like a time bomb,
Santos suddenly has something worth dying...
and worth living for.

On sale February.

Guardians

Protectors of the innocent...

SNEF07